# ALICE

Stevie B

Illustrated by Steven Krakow

Book layout by

Antonio Carlos Silva Filho

Croatian language coaching
provided by Anja

*This is a work of fiction. All of the characters, organizations, and events portrayed in this novel are either products of the author's imagination or are used fictitiously.*

ALICE



ISBN: 9798824008821

**Also by Stevie B**

*The Freaky Fungal Family Tree*

*Pajamas on a Sun Stained Beach*

www.thestevieb.com

# Contents

# Preface

Having been blessedly and gainfully involved in the entertainment industry for over a half-century, I have more than a vague understanding of how the principles of international copyright law work in regard to; copyright duration, works in the public domain, right to fair use, and use for parody. Thus, I felt comfortable employing ideas created in the mid-nineteen century as the foundation for this work before you. If I'm wrong, have your attorney contact my attorney and we'll fight it out in court. Because for me, this is a story I must tell, and in my opinion, it is well worth fighting for.

Alice is a Croatian immigrant working her ass off digging out of the debt incurred during the COVID-19 pandemic when food and beverage establishments were forced to shutter windows and lock their doors for many months. Patrons were far from the only ones feeling the effect of the lockdown. The impact on the millions of hardworking people worldwide formerly engaged at those establishments which provided employment for anyone willing to toil harder than most for minimum wage plus tips was, to say the least, devastating.

With income cut off as if someone had flipped a light switch, and if they were fortunate enough to have a credit score that allowed them credit cards, most walked a tightrope from billing statements to billing statements. With no other choice at hand, many sunk into massive debt that was bundled with the added burden of astronomical interest fees. My fictitious Alice was of the multitude that fell down that rabbit hole and was struggling to do her best to escape.

There is so much written between the lines of this tale that I hope I haven't buried the carrots so deep within the soil of fantasy that they go unfound. As any White Rabbit who's worth his weight in lucky rabbit feet (a phrase that must be ironic from the point of view of any rabbit who hears it and possessed a keen affection and affinity for irony), would tell you if rabbits could talk, those hidden carrots are well worth the digging.

In the course of offering up some of my own whimsical religious beliefs, I've not intended to disparage anyone else's view of what brought us all into existence. And that is something I'd be happy to swear on a stack of bibles, your honor. We'll just leave it at everything is what it is, until it just ain't anymore.

The truth behind my intentions is I hope to make you laugh, cry, feel, and most of all, think about what it really means to be alive. While I'm tempted to quote that iconic line from the film "The Sixth Sense" to prepare you for what you're about to read, I prefer to digress at this point and allow you to figure out what you need to figure out on your own. Come on, you're smart enough! I not only believe in the intelligence of my readers but also in our human spirit to embrace the wisdom of being kind to each other—and in doing good always.

Now bless you, my children, and let this adventure begin…

*So, shall we commence to sally forth?*

MAD

# Chapter I

# The Looking–Glass Crash

Oh, my goodness. Where's a girl's fairy godmother when she really needs her the most? Alice had just turned twenty-six and the eatery's staff where she worked (The Madd Hatter Bar & Restaurant located on Washington Street, Hobohemia's main drag), threw a small, surprise birthday party for her that night after closing. Twenty-six, yet somehow stuck waiting tables, deep in debt, tired as hell, still single, all alone, and now pregnant. This isn't where she saw herself eight years ago when she left high school. It wasn't the plan she or her parents had envisioned for her adulthood at all. Well, so much for plans, she figured. People planned—and God laughed up Her sleeve at the pathetic planners—as from afar, She watched their pitiable plots crumble and fail.

Alice's parents had instilled a strong sense of that good old fashion protestant work ethic embodied snugly within her psyche for as long as the girl could remember. At fourteen, they encouraged her to get a part-time job after school so she'd have her own pocket money, and told her; to work hard, save some of what she earned, and everything would turn out just fine. Only it wasn't fine.

After over a year of the COVID-19 lockdown, a year where it was no longer possible for a person to eke out their living by working gigs in the then universally shuttered food and beverage industry that provided employment for anyone willing to toil harder than most for minimum wage plus tips, her credit card debt had mounted as the months dragged by. Now, the total amount of interest charged each statement period on her accrued bills nearly equaled the required minimum payment requested. She fell deeper down the rabbit hole, which was a place so easy to fall into, once a person had gotten snared in 19.65% to 26.40% APR interest fees. The principals and fees seemingly compounded and grew uncontrollably every month on each of Alice's Visa, Master, American Express, and Discover credit cards.

The Madd Hatter's late-night "tea party" which had included a single round of drinks (compliments of the night manager) and a birthday cake with a solitary, solemn candle, that as obliged by tradition, she blew out minutes before the event had broken up. Perhaps because it was her birthday, her night manager, who usually could be a bit of a testy Jabberwock, had not only treated everyone to a free drink, he also had surprised her with a birthday present: an extra shift to work tomorrow.

So, instead of staying to party with her colleagues any longer, Alice unplugged the Segway ES2 electric scooter she kept in the back charging up while working her shifts to make the tedious trip from Hobohemia to the studio apartment she could barely afford in Brooklyn. Because the Jabberwocky's gift of an added shift entailed coming in to open the eatery tomorrow morning in order to work a double throughout the day and into the end of the night.

During daylight hours, the magic of light, in addition to various experiments with dyes and tints, could make the long hair she kept tied behind her while working appear as a fiery shade of deep titan red. Then, at other times, especially during dusk, it seemed to be somewhat flaxen and more strawberry blonde. This was not unlike her eyes, which looked to be either green or hazel color depending upon the time of day. The hair was her crowning glory (no pun intended). In fact, when not at the restaurant, Alice got gigs as a dancer in various music videos and worked using a stage name: Gingy. She loved listening and dancing to Afro-Fusion music (styles ranging from Coupé Décalé to Ndomboloto to Grawa-Grawa…) and was the go-to girl when many of the NYC production companies required dancers who possessed that rare look and unique talent. After collecting it tightly beneath the helmet of the protective headgear she normally adorned for these scooter rides, Alice picked up her share of the day's pooled tips prior to setting off into the warm early summer darkness.

Before leaving the Madd Hatter Bar & Restaurant (which sometimes felt like her own personal purgatory) she stole one last glance at the bright white face of the gothic-style clock hanging on the wall behind the bar, making a casual mental note that it was 3:15 AM. Oddly, as she turned away from the timepiece, Alice could have almost sworn that the hands of the tired ticker had begun to move precariously backward. Now that couldn't have been explained by the one drink she'd had. Due to her newly confirmed and unplanned pregnancy, she'd only imbibed a cup of cranberry juice *sans* any addition of alcohol instead of her usual glass of Dos

Minas Malbec red wine. Well, maybe it was just—oh well—never mind…

The ride home on *Crvena Plesačica* (her name for the scooter, which in English meant The Red Dancer) always began down Washington Street, was at first unproblematic. As it was Alice's wont, as well as the fact that the two-wheeler's maximum velocity was limited to about 16 mph even with a strong tailwind, she drove cautiously below the legal speed limit through the sparse nighttime vehicular traffic. That was until the front wheel of the Segway ES2 sank down deep into one of the many potholes that plagued pedestrians and drivers on Hobohemian streets and sidewalks alike. Frightfully, this caused her to swerve slightly toward the direction of a van parked streetside.

And yet again, another odd optical illusion had occurred that evening. Alice saw the scooter's lone headlight, as well as the image of her upon it, heading in her direction before she crashed straight into the parked carrier. Well, at least this time, it was a phenomenon that could be naturally and rationally explained. For you see, festooned along its sides were unframed sheets of glass and mirrors. Then, the last thing Alice remembered, after flying up and over the handlebar, was going headlong and helmet first into and through the looking-glass!

*...headlong*

*and*

*helmet*

*first*

*into*

*and*

*through*

*the*

*looking-glass!*

# Chapter II

## Alice's Garden of Flowers

After the accident, when Alice finally regains consciousness, she was in the bar standing before the aforementioned gothic-looking clock that read one minute before 9 AM in the morning. This time the timepiece's hands are definitely ticky-tocky headed backward in the counterclockwise all wrong direction.

"Just speak in Croatian when you can't think of the English words for a thing. Turn around a time or two, then walk away, and remember who you are, Alice!" said Naida as she hopped down off the top of the bar. She'd been adorning the interior of The Madd Hatter Bar & Restaurant with flowers she had fashioned out of *papier-mâché* (because, if anyone would ever care to ask her, she'd tell them that the Madd owners of the Hatter do not care about such matters). Somehow and whatnot, Naida appeared definitely different from what Alice could remember. No—it couldn't be—could it?

"Naida, dear, did you do something different with your hair?" Alice asked.

Yet, no, it wasn't just her friend's hair, but everything about her was, well, somewhat off. There now were two tiny pointed ears atop her head. They were barely visible, but Alice was sure they were ears nonetheless. A sheen of fine hairs coated Naida's face, so much so, that it resembled fur. What was more out of place were the long whiskers she now sported from the mid-sides of her cheeks, which extended well above and past each adjacent shoulder. Then most peculiar of all was that—oh Holy Mother who art in heaven, hallowed be thy name—shall she dare even think it? As Alice's eyes traveled the short distance between her friend's shoulders, down past her arms— Naida's hands now looked like paws—and instead of fingernails, they were tipped with small, sharp claws.

"Naida? It's been wizards' years since I've heard that name. Everyone here, of course, currently calls me Dinah. So, you may call me Dinah now as well, dear."

As she expressed her preference in the appellation, Naida/Dinah lifted her right paw to her lips, giving the white and black fur on the back of it a few licks with the flat, long, broad tongue that flicked out from her pink lips. Satisfied that the paw was then sufficiently suited for the job she had in mind, she used it to thoroughly groom the back of each of the ears that now crowned her cranium. First, she brushed the right ear, and then reaching around, toiled with the left one until sure the task had been adequately accomplished. Oh, my moons and stars, thought Alice—should she even think it—much less say? And if she were to say it, then how shall it be kindly said? Well…might as well just get it out there then—the girl who's her very, very, very good friend—presently looked just like—a cat!

Now, it wasn't so out of sorts for Alice's gal pal to play a joke on someone, although it was rarely on Alice. During the time they worked in the restaurant together, which often would seem an eternity, customers had frequently remarked how similar the two looked, and on occasion, even questioned if they were sisters. So, the girls, girls being girls, colluded on a prank when asked by replying they were not only sisters but indeed twins. They'd even concocted a tale where they'd been born to Russian parents who were on the run from some bad guys back in the old country. Thus, their parents had forbidden them to speak Russian in public, lest they'd blow the family's cover. Most of those who'd inquired about their biological connection ate this up like an overweight person tasting their first French fry. As a matter of fact, many of the inquisitive customers had nicknamed them The Russian Dolls. You know, the kind where you open up one to find another smaller one inside, then a smaller one inside of that one that had a smaller one inside that had the next smaller one inside, so on, and so forth, a hay penny and sixpence as they heard some from across the pond would remark.

Trying to avoid it, yet ultimately yielding to temptation, Alice broached the subject to ask, "Naida, sorry, I meant Dinah, are you, are you, well I don't know how to say it, so I'll just blurt out, are you a cat?"

"Am I a cat?"

"A cat, a feline, a moggie, a puss, a kitty, a mouser, a tabby, a grimalkin, a pussy, a malkin, a…?"

“A cat? Alice dear girl, what exactly are you trying to say?”

“I’m actually no longer quite sure now, Nai… I mean, my dear Dinah. I’m presently at such a loss for words, I guess is where I’m at on this touchy-touchy tabby subject.”

“Then simply do as I instructed earlier of trying to say it in Croatian instead of English. We’ll see if that’s the remedy for this illness.”

Alice then uttered, “*Da li si zaista mačka*?” prior to turning around a time or two, then walking away and remembering who she was.

“Oh, I understand you now. You’re asking if I’m a…”

It was exactly then that one of the *papier-mâché* flowers rudely interrupted their conversation.

“Of course, she’s a blithering cat, you boob! We may not have real eyes, but even all of us hanging here can see that.”

“Me too.”

“Yeah, me too.”

“Me too.”

“And me too.”

The “me toos” continued as the chorus went on and on until each and every flustered flower had eventually chimed in on that touchy feline subject.

“Who said that?” Alice boldly asked as she spun around on her toes to see and hear who was saying what. “Speak up now, who?”

“I said that,” someone after a few seconds had contritely confessed.

“May I ask your name then, in order that I may address you properly?”

“Well, obviously, it’s Rose, my child,” replied the blood-red *papier-mâché* flower.

“Well, Rose, that was a tad impolite of you to interrupt others in the midst of a very serious discussion. And then to add insult to the injury, as if to pour salt on the wound, you called me a boob!”

Oh,” Rose said with a sigh, “I have been told on occasion I may be a might thorny at times. I apologize.”

“Then, apology accepted, if for no other reason than many believe that to hold a grudge for too long may be bad for one’s health.”

“I then apologize too,” said another, then another and another until every *papier-mâché* flower in the place said they were sorry.

“Alright, now that we’ve put a rest to that may I inquire as to your names?” asked Alice.

In accordance, each and every freaky faux flower identifies itself. There was Daisy, one named Tiger-lily, Sweet Pea, another called herself Violet, Azalea, the ever so shy Begonia, the overly curious Chrysanthemum, even a Dahlia, and too, too, too many to remember if not written down. And Alice was way too busy listening to write anything down even if she’d possessed pencil and paper, and Dinah would be of no help seeing she had pussy paws as opposed to human hands. So, what was Alice left to do but listen? She remembered she was told, “Talk less – listen more!” Which in and of itself wasn’t much of a plan, but when it’s the only plan available, one must make do with what one has…

***Of***
***course,***
***she's***
***a***
***blithering***
***cat,***
***you***
***boob!***

# Chapter III

## Insects We Trust

—

## Now Get Your Minds Out of the Gutter

By this time, Dinah had climbed atop one of the barstools within The Madd Hatter Bar & Restaurant. She sat upon it much as a cat would; her lean, long legs were pulled up before her with pawed arms clasped around them, resting her furred chin on her kneecaps, while Alice and the fluent flowers spoke more. Finding this of little interest, she slowly lowered the lids of her eyes to enjoy a quick morning catnap, sank into a dream about having a hit or two of catnip, chasing some mice about the restaurant's kitchen, and contently purred herself to sleep.

But the mice in this dream did not play by the rules. Each time she would corner one in the kitchen, it would turn into an insect. Now, not your average insect, mind you, but very, very, very large insects. So large: larger than a cat, even larger than the many lions of the African jungles who were her distant cousins. Ergo, much, much, much larger than herself, so much so that they not only gave her a start and a fright but when cornered, would turn about to chase the cagey kitty. Oh, the irony of the hunter being now the hunted. The irony, indeed! The last thing any cat could want to be called was "a scaredy cat."

Awaking with a sudden, startled shutter of her lithely Molly body, Dinah checked the clock above the bar for the time. Since the turned around ticker had been ticky-tocking backward, it was now around 6:21 AM, so she still had some Z time, 3 hours, 21 minutes, and 1 second to be precise, to nod off again. Especially since Alice and those talkative flowers had ceased their babbling. So, she decided to close her pussycat eyes for another snooze until 3 AM, which was closing time for the MHB&R. And since time was now moving backward, at precisely one second past 2:59 and 59 seconds in the nocturnal morning, the place would be open again so that she, and Alice, and the other waitstaff would be working another shift. This time when Dinah dozed, as the flowers had done with Alice, the interestingly big insects spoke to her to offer an apology.

"We're sorry, luv, didn't mean to give you such a start. It's just that we can never trust when we'll be changed in size, now can we, hon?" said one of the beetles about the size of a large buffalo.

Then an enormous ephemerid chipped in, "Yeah, our bad, babe!"

Well, what do you know? The insects actually appeared to be rather nice. But cats being cats, Dinah was still unsure if they were worthy of her trust.

A mantis that had been praying on the floor now added, "We all could've handled that better, lass. We really could have, should have, and would have—if we only had a clue—before these changes occur. But we just don't, so there you have it, and there it is, I guess."

The sensuously slumbering puss noticed the mantis was

holding a bible (she believed it to be the New King James version, but cats probably know as much about bibles as fish know how to ride bicycles), so she ventured to ask, “Would you all swear to that on the bible he’s holding?”

“We will,” they agreed in unison as each placed a hand or a foot or whatever (it’s rather difficult to tell which is which with bugs) and spoke the following words as one like they were some sort of Greek chorus; “We shouldn’t have did what we did when we did do what we did to you. We’re sorry, kitty cat.”

Taking this act of attrition perhaps too much at face value, but sincerely taking it to heart, the kindly kitten recalled what Alice had told the talkative funny flowers of how holding a grudge for too long may be bad for one’s health. So simply seconds prior to waking again, the un-begrudging grimalkin forgave one and all and then awoke. Groggily, Dinah lustily stretched her body, you know, in the feline-ish fashion cats are prone to do when they wake, to get ready to work another night shift at The Madd Hatter Bar & Restaurant. Oh, oh, oh, what a wickedly wild shift it would be. And here, we shift you not…

***We shouldn't***
***have did***
***what we did***
***when we***
***did do***
***what we did***
***to you.***

# Chapter IV

## Tweedle Me This Then Tweedle Me That

The Jabberwocky, also known as the night manager at The Madd Hatter Bar & Restaurant, was in his office that night interviewing a pair of rather heavyset ladies for positions at the food and beverage establishment. One of the prospects was named Dee, and the other called herself Dom, which of course, were abbreviated first names of Desiree and Dominique. But the interview was going far from well.

When he inquired by asking as to their qualification, "Are you experienced…", and prior to the inclusion of a position to be filled, the opening bars of Jimi Hendrix and the Experience's "Purple Haze" blasted from nowhere to blare out his voice. On the second attempt asking "Are you experienced…" he was drowned out by the band's "Manic Depression." Next came "Hey, Joe," followed by "Love or Confusion," "May This Be Love," "I Don't Live Today," "The Wind Cries Mary," "Fire," "Third Stone from the Sun," "Foxy Lady," and wrapping it up with a rousing rendition of "Are You Experienced."

Now, if there was one thing that Alice was unquestionably quite sure of, it was her Hendrix! And that this must be the American version of the classic hard rock album. Because she knew the one she was familiar with listening to while growing up in Croatia, the U.K. version would've contained the following Side-One sequence: "Foxy Lady," "Manic Depression," "Red House," "Can You See Me," "Love or Confusion," "I Don't Live

Today," followed by Side Two's "May This Be Love," "Fire," "Third Stone from the Sun," "Remember," and "Are You Experienced."

After hearing the American version upon arriving in her newly adopted USA homeland, she'd thought of what a travesty that the European edition had neglected to include neither "Purple Haze," nor "Hey, Joe," or even "The Wind Cries Mary." What a travesty, indeed! In the woman's humble opinion, those were the three best tracks from any of Hendrix's earlier ethereal and epic song catalogs. Although, they at least did maintain "Foxy Lady" in their messed-up, myopic, and misguided Euro mix.

Time after time, the Jabberwocky would repeat his question to Dee and Dom only to be drowned out by the power trio's blistering brand of rock & roll.

"Dee, are you experienced with...", or, "Dom, are you experienced in…" but before he could fully get out what he was attempting to ask, Jimi's gut-punching guitar riffed over him. "Ba-bump…Ba-bump... Bump-ba-ba-baaaaaaaa-ba-da-ba-baaaa. Bump-bump-bum-baaaaaaaa, ba-da-da,daaaaaaaa... Ba-da-ba-baaaaaaaa-ba-da-ba-baaaa, Ba-da-ba-baaaaaaaa-ba-da-ba…" which was cut short by Hendrix's shrieking lyrics, "Purple haze, all in my brain…" Or, "Manic depression is searching my soul…" Or the lyrics from any of the other nine songs on the American mix.

"*Oh, sranje!" - Što se dovraga događa*?" Alice thought to herself in her native tongue, which of course, when translated to English, would be, "Oh, shit! What the hell is happening?", as she and Dinah listened to the exchange from outside his office door while the two of them stood so still you would probably forget that they were still alive.

"*Ne znam. Možda se zabavljaju ili nešto*" Dinah replied, and which if you go ask Alice, she'd explain that was Croatian for, "I don't know. Perhaps they're rocking out or something."

"Dinah! When did you learn to speak my language?"

"We've always spoken the same language, sis. It's just sometimes we do it in different tongues."

"Oh, all right then. I guess that makes a lot of sense in some kind of curiously convoluted way. It's just that recently my head hurts because not much is really making sense at all." As she spoke those last words, Alice rubbed her forehead, and much to her surprise, a bump had now risen where she touched, even though she couldn't remember hitting her head on anything. This had now become as bizarre and strange as those Marvel comics she'd read in secret as a child in Croatia; comic books that had first led her to learn how to read and speak the English language.

By this time, the Jabberwocky had now thrown in the towel of defeat on his questions. Taking advantage of his sudden silence, first Dee and then followed by Dom, each recited a poem.

Dee's, was rather short:

Tweedle me this then tweedle me that
Agree to tweedle and twaddle
For tweedle me this then tweedle me that
Been so bored by all your prattle
Just what you say it matters not
As you ask of our experience
Ponder this then ponder that
What makes you so f-ing curious?

Feverishly Alice tried to transcribe what she thought she was hearing. But neither by listening to, or reading them, could the women make out any of the words. It was all just gibberish. So, turning to Dinah for advice, Alice asked, "Was she speaking Pig Latin, or could it be Esperanto, or ancient Aramaic or something? Does any of this make a lick of sense to you, dear sister?"

"Meow, I mean, not really, meow. But then you could ask the looking-glass, my sister, meow."

She had never been aware of the cracked mirror that hung

from the wall next to the Jabberwocky's door. Figuring there was nothing to lose, she held up the meandering and meaningless scrawled text so it could be reflected in the glass, then queried boisterously, "Mirror, mirror, on the wall. Do you understand this hot mess at all?"

But the mirror only stared back at Alice in glassy silence. Looking intently into its reflection, then seeing the words, letters, and lines in reverse of what she had hurriedly jotted down, their meaning now gently emerged like an early rising of each morning's sun.

Tweedle me this then tweedle me that

Agree to tweedle and twaddle

For tweedle me this then tweedle me that

Been so bored by all your prattle

Just what you say it matters not

As you ask of our experience

Ponder this then ponder that

What makes you so f-ing curious?

While on the other hand, or paw if you were Dinah, Dom's poem was rather tediously long. It went on, stanza after stupid stanza, rattling and ranting about some wacky walrus walking around with some capricious carpenter and their penchant for procuring oysters to devour. Much too long if one were to retell the telling of it here, so shall we all just agree, for the sake of brevity, to carry on to carry this trippy tale forward to the next detail? Can we? Good, it appears it's now unanimous that we merely move this yarn along. If there is a next part, which of course there is. That is if no one is readily prepared to read the usual parting pair of words handily bandied about in literature. You know: "The End." Words that are typically, and traditionally, employed to wrap up most stories you'll read. Well, that will occur here too, but just not quite yet…

*Are*

*you*

*experienced...*

# Chapter V

## Wooly Waters of Woe

Time to kick out the jams, and get going, in full gear! After the discovery of the bump on her bean, Alice was having a trying time recalling the events that led to her prior morning presence in The Madd Hatter Bar & Restaurant only a few hours ago. Also, why was the clock moving backward, and Naida (it was so a task getting used to now calling her Dinah), why had her "sister" transmogrified into a name-changing cat? In addition, what was this magic mysteriously associated with mirrors? And let's not lose mind of the Jabberwocky who had fits of reoccurring hallucinogenic Hendrix horrors, those freakish flowers, Dee and Dom, or all the other tidbits of weirdness clouding her mind that she'd encountered within the past several hours.

Mentally, it now felt as if she were a percipient prisoner who had not only been imprisoned prior to a court judgment but in advance of committing any crime. Was she losing her marbles? Around Alice, everyone now was conversing in riddles and rhymes. It was simply senseless. What would happen next is all she wanted to know.

At that very moment, all the music and the chatter of customers, kitchen crew, and waitstaff alike had come to a close as silence now prevailed within the walls of the MHB&R. Turning about on the balls of her feet, she saw the reason why. The Madd Hatter himself, and his wife, the Redd Queen, the owners of the joint, had just entered the place. Everything there within came to a screeching standstill. Something, indeed, was undoubtedly up.

The Hatter and the Queen rarely came in, that is, unless there was a problem. And if there was a problem, you never wanted to be the problem they had a problem with. Silently thinking to herself, Alice thought, now this is certainly going to be a waste of time.

Spinning on his heels, the Hatter trapped her with his stare and rudely reprimanded, “If you knew time only half as well as we do, then you wouldn’t be babbling like a brain-dead brook about it!”

With a gasp of amazement that the Madd man had the ability to hear anyone’s thoughts, the frightened fem responded, “I didn’t think…”

“Listen, missy. If you don’t think, then you shouldn’t be talking. That’s the problem with your kind; you’re forever going on about things you don’t know.” Turning to the Queen, he queried, “My, my, my, my, my, my… What shall we do with such an unruly one?”

“Off with her head!” wailed his wife.

“But I’ve done nothing, sir,” then believing it wise, she added, “and madam.”

“Well, if you’re doing nothing, then why are we paying

you?"

"Oh, I, I, I… You really don't pay us that very much, sir, for all the work we do."

"This girlie sounds basically bonkers," the Queen and Hatter sang out together, "are you bonkers, missy?"

"Alright, well, that is an excellent question, and I'm so happy you asked because I must say, as of late, I'll admit to feeling somewhat off-kilter or something."

"There she goes again! She's not thinking but thinks she should talk about what she's thinking even when the girl has no useful thoughts to share," the bullying proprietor proclaimed.

"Off with her head!"

"Now," spoke the Hatter, "I'll ask only one last time, are you bonkers?"

"Because anyone is bonkers is no reason to treat someone with any less respect. I mean, some of the best brains in history were considered to be bonkers, so…"

"Oh, no, this one is most surely and certifiably bonkers, my dear."

"Off with her head!"

Getting up and into her grill, the Hatter bellowed, "Why are all of you just standing around gathering wool as you rob us blind by stealing money from us while doing nothing? You cheat, you lie, and you drink all the water you want from our faucets without paying us a single cent for it. It's a disgrace! And if you are unabashedly bonkers, we certainly can't keep you here since the health insurance we so generously provide for every single employee doesn't cover that, now, can we?"

"But, meow, you don't, meow, provide any, meow, insurance for anyone, meow, here, meow, sir," now spoke Dinah.

"Off with her head!"

"Liar! And who brought this cat into my restaurant? The board of health inspectors would certainly have a field day if they caught us with this mangy fleabag using our divine diner as her personal and very fine five-star litter box. Was it you?" he beseeched of Alice.

"To be honest, sir, she was already here when I arrived. Not only that, she's Naida. You remember Naida, don't you, sir?"

"Who?"

"Naida."

"Who?"

"Dinah?"

"Who?"

“She’s one of the best workers you have here, working harder than most would for what you pay us along with tips!”

“Who?”

Bonkers or not, Alice wordlessly wondered to herself, “*Je li netko pustio sovu unutra?*” or in English, “Had someone let an owl slip into this place?”

“I heard that! And not only is my name not Al, but I own this very place, that is, along with my wonderful wife,” the Hatter hollered.

“Meow, meow, meow, meow…”

“Someone remove this cat from the premises. Get it out the door, and into the street, now!”

“Off with her head!”

And with that, The Madd Hatter Bar & Restaurant bouncers, who also acted as security for the boss and his wife, led Dinah away and through the door. There was nothing left of the cat but its mischievous, toothy, girlish grin, which remained hanging in the air. After that, everyone seemed to dissipate and disappear like a drop of water atop a red hot grill. That is, all except Alice. Leaving the woman alone in the room with a throbbing headache, wondering and worrying if she’d ever see her sweet “sister” again…

*...are*

*you*

***bonkers, missy?***

BOOK

# Chapter VI

## Dumpty Humpty Hi-Dee-Ho

The cockeyed clock now read 10:34 PM when Alice went back into the packed barroom area of the Hatter. Taking a moment before returning to work, she stood in a corner and faced the wall, then just lost it and began crying after the dreadful events that had just occurred. Tears now streamed down her pretty cheeks in care and concern for her recently departed friend. She really did need to get it together, get it together quickly, and return to work.

But before she could turn about to leave the corner, she felt the sensation of gentle gyrations, like someone was rubbing their pelvic region against her delicate *derrière*. Turning around and right before getting ready to smack some sense into the offending predator, she saw it was Frank, one of the MHB&R regulars. Any woman who worked there knew Frank well. A few had even dubbed him Frottage Frank because he was what they called a "close talker" and was far too touchy-feely.

Alice wasn't sure if the story was true, but she'd heard from another worker a twisted tale about him. It happened before her tenure of working at this place. Apparently, some other girl made the mistake of accepting his offer to go out for dinner. Toward the end of the meal, he whipped out his wallet and removed something laminated. Frank told her it was his VIP membership card for an exclusive, private club catering to the golden shower crowd called Wee The People, and they should go for after-dinner drinks. The girl freaked out, excused herself to use the restroom, and then made a hasty retreat out the back to get as far away from him as possible. Nearly as bad, this public pervert was a pitifully poor tipper.

"Frank, what are you doing?"

"Oh, Alice, I didn't know that was you, sorry! Can you grab me another Bud Light, sweetheart, and just add it to my tab? I won't get paid until next week. Oh—wait a minute—it's my birthday today!"

Tab, now that's a big fat joke! Frank had no tab because he was the Redd Queen's brother, which by marriage made him the Madd Hatter's brother-in-law. So he never paid for anything. When it came to tipping, no matter how much he'd consumed during his visit he'd usually leave only a coin or two that he had jangling about in his pocket, along with a below-average alibi of taking care of the server the next time he dropped in.

It wasn't that Frank was such a bad egg as far as anyone could tell; he was generally just gross, cheap, smelly, overly obese, and annoying. Besides, he had a reputation for drinking so much he'd sometimes fall from his barstool and couldn't get off the floor. Thus, they'd have to pick him up and put him back together again, so to speak, then set him up on his stool where he could just fall off another time.

Frank would also try to scam the staff into thinking it was his birthday at least once a month or more. This was done in order to then make the argument that it was The Madd Hatter Bar & Restaurant's unwritten policy to serve free drinks to anyone on their birthday. Which was not true, but when the Madd Hatter himself found out about the un-birthday drinks, he'd dock the pay of the unlucky soul who'd served those.

One time after Naida had brought him countless rounds he left only thirteen pennies atop the bar and then departed. Now, Naida had a hot temper, no one could deny that, but it really took a lot for anyone to get under her skin and up her craw enough to completely blow her top. But that night, after seeing the miserly, measly amount of the gratuity, she lost it! Grabbing the pennies, she rushed out the door to toss the coins in his face. But alas, Frottage Frank must've already rounded the corner and was nowhere to be found. For a fat man, he could move swiftly when necessary. It was probably just as well she hadn't pelted him with his pittance because she really needed this gig and that fat fracker wasn't worth losing her job over.

Okay, now that we've lifted the lid on the topic of regulars, perhaps we've opened the door enough to dish some more. Some were normal, some were not, and some were not so normal but not so much as to be a pain in the poor old *derrière,* like Frank. As a matter of fact, she spotted one such individual drinking at the bar and reading a book, even though, in her opinion, it was too dark to read without hurting your eyes. This guy was somewhat of a mystery to most of the staff, although generally assessed to be of no harm.

After getting Frank his un-birthday beer, she went over to speak to the bookworm and said, “Hey, you’ll never know what a crazy mixed-up night I’ve had so far, and there’re many miles to still travel before I’m out of here. You won’t believe some of…”

Stopping short as she spoke, she stared at the barroom reader. As with Naida after morphing into Dinah, he too had ears atop his head. Unlike her “sister’s” perky little ones, his were much longer and rather floppy. As with her dearly departed friend, he was covered in fur, although whereas her “sis’s” pelt was white with random splotches of black here and there, his was simply a solid snow white. Another similarity to Dinah was he too had paws instead of hands. May She who art in Heaven help me, thought Alice, he looks exactly like a White Rabbit!

The book reading bunny rested his novel on the bar and looked at her with recognition of their past meetings. The irises of the White Rabbit’s eyes were a burning pink color, much like a summer sunset at a beach. Oddly, she took note that he now had a gold pocket watch attached to a long chain fob. Something she’d never seen him sport before.

“Are you OK?” he asked Alice with care and concern.

“I’m not really sure, and maybe I’ve just gone insane, but I keep on getting this feeling that something’s not right with the world, at least not this world.”

“This world? Well, that sounds more interesting than the book I’m reading, so why don’t you just tell me everything about it? I’m all ears!”

Then as if to buy more time prior to concluding whether she felt comfortable enough to confide in him, she stalled by asking, “Why are you always reading when you’re at our bar?”

“Now, Alice, the reasons are threefold. One: It helps to discourage most people from speaking to me. But you, I like and feel comfortable with, and I’m happy when we talk, so, present company excluded. Two: With these ears, I’m able to hear much of everything, but with my poor eyesight, every day it’s become increasingly difficult to see what’s around me, which is why I wear these glasses. Since I fear I’ll eventually go blind I take every opportunity to read whenever I can while still able. Three: Books are my mask. They allow me to surreptitiously study everything from behind them, take mental notes, then hop home and write about what I’ve observed. For instance, the idea of looking around is ludicrous since you may only look backward, or forward, or right to left at the same moment. But unless one has a pair of eyes on each side of the head and another pair at the back, well, no one may truly look around all at once. One, two, three, four, easy-peasy-lemon-squeezy!”

Her female intuition told Alice she could probably trust him. So, first checking if any of her managers were watching, she sidled into the barstool next to the White Rabbit, took a leap of faith, and began to pour out her crazy heart to him…

***...it's***
***my***
***birthday***
***today!***

# Chapter VII

## The Lion
## Ate
## My Unicorn

The White Rabbit listened attentively to every detail Alice described to him. Because she was still on the clock (not the one which was mysteriously moving backward but the one she and the other employees were required to punch ahead of each shift), she spoke rather rapidly and excited. Once she felt she had successfully relayed an encapsulated version of all the events she'd endured, and when all had been said on what had been done, Alice was breathlessly out of breath. She was also thankfully relieved to have had someone to lend an ear to listen to her confusion. And when it came to ears, the White Rabbit was no slouch. Placing the paw of his right arm on her shoulder, the hare gave it a fatherly squeeze of support.

"Well, that's pretty much everything to tell, I imagine. What do you believe I should do?" asked Alice.

"I imagine you should first take a breath. Then take another, and another, followed by another, and then just keep breathing. Next, I believe when you bounce off this barstool, you should place one foot in front of the other to take one step after another, and another, followed by another, then just keep on keeping on until you've thought this fully through."

Taking the bunny's first bit of advice, she inhaled, then exhaled, then inhaled again, and so on and so forth, and thankfully, it did make her feel somewhat better. During the time Alice had been catching her breath, he had taken out the gold pocket watch and flipped open its lid to see the time.

"Holy cabbage and carrots!" he gasped, "I'm late! I'm late, for a very important date!" then sprung off his barstool and hopped out of the Madd Hatter Bar & Restaurant door to go wherever he had to go before it got much later.

Have any of you ever thought about this: One can't really catch one's breath since our breaths are only air, and as with the wind, it's impossible to hold it in your hands or trap it in a snare? And has anyone ever seen time as it goes by and about us? Well, I think not. Now, this is not to say that that which you cannot catch and hold and that which cannot be seen is not there. What's been stated has simply been said to set the record straight so we may continue to sally forth in this story. Okay?

Stepping from the barstool, Alice proceeded to do as the clever cottontail had instructed, placing one foot in front of the other to take one step after another. But before our heroine had gone too far, she bumped right into the Jabberwocky coming out of his office, who said without a please or a thank you, "Alice, go on down to the storage cellar for mushrooms then take them up to the kitchen."

Since arguing with him was like dancing in a minefield, one had to choose carefully. So, from the night manager's door, down the stairs to the cellar, then over to an area where the

MHB&R stowed mushrooms, she was struck by a surprising sight. You see, upon the largest mushroom in the lot, which was a very, very, very large mushroom indeed, Alice spied a very, very, very large caterpillar atop the colossal cap of the meaty mushroom. Now that, in and by itself was weird. But what was even weirder wasn't that the larval Lepidoptera was sitting there with his eyes closed. It was that the caterpillar was smoking a very, very, very large hookah!

"Who are you?" the startled server loudly exclaimed!

"Jeff. Just Jeff."

"Jeff who?"

"Just Jeff, I need no other name for I'm not fish, or fowl, nor game. Although I'm not like other people, I'm someone, just the same. So please, it's Just Jeff, for Just Jeff's my only name."

"You're a caterpillar!"

"No, I'm Just Jeff, but okay, you may have it your way too."

"Just Jeff, what are you doing?"

"Obviously, I'm taking a hit off this hookah. Would you like one too? I'm happy to share, happy to share with you."

Handing the nozzle-tipped tube which was attached to the base of the hookah over to Alice, she held it gently but firmly in her soft hands and was surprised by how warm and rigid the length of it was to the touch, then took a second or two to think of what she should do.

"Oh, Just Jeff, I know not what to do!"

"Take a hit; take a hit, perhaps a hit or two?"

"You know, Just Jeff, considering all that I've been through, why in Heaven's name not? Perhaps it could alleviate the pain from this headache which seems to have gotten worse. What could possibly go wrong?"

Taking his long hard nozzle between her tender, slightly parted, soft red lips (again: get your minds out of the gutter!), she inhaled deeply. The smoke and vapor from the pipe filled her lungs. Hey, it wasn't so bad. It really wasn't so bad at all.

"Hold it in, hold it in, then let it out to do it all again. Blink your eyes, first once, then twice. What comes next is really, really nice."

Being a good girl, Alice did as she was told. And in fact, it did seem to relieve the pain and throbbing from her headache somewhat. But then, something most strange ensued. You see, she and the caterpillar began to grow to an enormous size. So big that between the two of them, there wasn't a single inch of space left unfilled by their bodies within the huge, cavernous cellar. The two were so squish-squashed together that for the second time in a very short while, Alice again found it somewhat difficult to breathe.

"Just Jeff! What's just happened?"

"We grew, and grew, and grew. But worry not, the growing's stopped, now dream of what you'd like to do."

So, Alice dreamt that they could be freed from this cramped cellar. When she opened her eyes anew and emerged from her dream, she was upstairs sitting on the barstool she had sat upon merely minutes before. More amazing than that, Just Jeff was behind the bar serving drinks to anyone who ordered. Only now, he looked more like a man than a caterpillar and was rocking a martini shaker with both hands above his head.

"What can I get you?" he asked Alice.

"Well, I'm not really thirsty. Right now, after the last twelve hours, I believe I need a miracle. You wouldn't happen to have a unicorn behind that bar, would you?"

"Sorry, but we're all out of the unicorn today."

"Whatever happened to the unicorn?"

"Oh, the lion ate the unicorn."

"Why did the lion eat the unicorn?"

"Perhaps it was just because the unicorn was not able to run quicker than the lion, and fast enough to get away to not be eaten."

"Uhmmm, that also would explain a lot now, wouldn't it?"

As odd as that sounded to Alice, it made a lot more sense than much of what had happened to her so far. It could also be an explanation as to why we no longer see unicorns anymore…

***Sorry,***
***but we're***
***all out***
***of the***
***unicorn***
***today***

# Chapter VIII

## I Get A Kick Out of You

After hearing the disheartening news of what had happened to the last Madd Hatter Bar & Restaurant unicorn, Alice looked up at the whacked-out clock above the bar to check the time. The hands had now moved back in time to 7:55 PM, and outside it was still daylight. Needing a tick or two after that news to readjust herself to the fact that it wasn't the morning sun rising—it was instead the sun that had unset—and then accepted yet another fact; there were no longer unicorns—and there would probably never be—any unicorns ever again.

"You know what I'm thinking now?" she asked Just Jeff behind the bar. "I'm thinking maybe I really don't need a unicorn. Anyways, I do have my electric scooter, and that gets me around and between towns exceedingly well."

'Twas then a third thought came to mind. Where was her Segway? Alice had no recollection of having ridden from her home in Brooklyn to where she worked here in Hobohemia, much less than leaving it in the back of the MHR&B to recharge in the area where she would always keep it plugged in. This was a most worrisome fact, but searching her memory for its whereabouts only encouraged the headache to return, and upon return, it felt far worse than before.

About to ask Just Jeff for the aspirin they stored behind the bar and hoping the lion had not eaten that too, a distraction occurred. A knight attired in a full suit of armor had entered, stood behind the first customer standing at the bar he encountered, and gave the man a swift kick in the *derrière*, nearly knocking the poor fellow across and over the top of the bar. The knight then moved to kick the next man, then the next, and then the next.

When he was finally behind Giuseppe, Giuseppe, who was known as a bit of a tough guy in and around the neighborhood, and who was there drinking with a few friends, the armored foot of the knight introduced itself to his vulnerable backside. When Giuseppe fell forward, he not only knocked over his own drink but some of his friend's drinks as well. Reflexively turning around to face the assaulter who had assaulted him, and to assault his assaulter in retribution, the tough guy posed a question.

"Hey, why you a'go and a'kick a'me in a'my bum, brother?"

The knight raised the visor of his helmet to reply, "Because I can."

"Oh yeah?"

"Yes. Turn around and I'll kick it again if you need a further demonstration."

Now, Giuseppe may have been a tough guy, but he was certainly not foolish enough to turn back around for yet another kick. Instead, he fisted a hand, pulled back his massive arm, and sent one of his infamous haymaker punches in the direction of the offender's face. But before his fist could land on it, the knight flipped down the helmet visor for protection. So, Giuseppe's hand smashed into the metal armor shielding the butt-kicker. Even from a few yards away, Alice heard some bones break in the tough guy's fingers and hand.

"Ahhhhhhhhhh!" he screamed in pain, then cradled the mangled metacarpus with his still healthy hand.

Giuseppe's friends helped him out of the bar and got the grimacing guy to a hospital for care.

It was then the knight turned in Alice's direction, gestured toward the helmet as he raised his visor once more, and spoke, "A helmet is a very good way to protect your crown, Alice, but you can't always be sure it will save you. Not even when one is crowned princess or queen." Returning the visor to its closed position, the knight retreated from the darkened Hatter to the now radiantly early evening sun shining outdoors and was gone as quick as he'd come.

His parting comment made Alice think that she not only couldn't remember what she'd done with her ES2; the waitress had nary an inkling as to where the protective headgear helmet she normally wore when riding her scooter had been deposited. With elbows on the bar, she now rested head in hands. The bump on her forehead was larger, tender, and she detected a somewhat sticky substance seeping from it. Removing the mitt from her head, in its palm, there now appeared to be a tiny drop of something red, like blood.

"Whatever do you believe he meant by that, Just Jeff?"

"Probably, just those invented innovations invented over the years, like helmets, come in rather handy when something is about to hurt your head."

"I mean the part about it won't always save you."

"Maybe that even when you believe you're fully protected, like the way you put your helmet on at the end of a day's shift to ride your scooter home, perhaps you're really not," answered the bartender that once was a caterpillar and then a man and who was now spinning and weaving a silk cocoon around himself.

"Just Jeff," Alice said with an earsplitting note of alarm in her voice, "Whatever are you doing now?"

The cocoon already around his body was now about to encase the face of Just Jeff's head, so he had to tell her sooner than later, "I'm changing for the last time, and after this change, I'll eventually die."

With a horrified gasp, the girl pleaded, "But I don't want you to die, Just Jeff. Please don't go and die!"

His voice, barely audible beneath the silken cocoon, was

now extremely muffled, so what words were spoken by the ever-changing bartender were the last words she or anyone else at the Hatter heard him say, "Alice, we don't live forever. Not you, nor me. And what's more, we don't always get what we want, and sometimes not even what we need. I imagine someone would have told you this by now, so perhaps I shall. Alice, when you last rode home, you hit a pothole, and now you're…"

But before he could share the message in full, his head was entirely encased in the silk that cut off his final words. For an amount of time that went unmeasured, she stared through the blur of her tears at Just Jeff's silken coffin. At first, she thought it was the distortion of those tears that created another optical illusion to trick her. A beautifully painted wing, followed by another, burst out from inside the cocoon, and what emerged was a lovely butterfly.

"Jeff, you're not dead yet! I'm so, so, so, very hap..."

And as with Just Jeff, Alice was left with unfinished words on her tongue as the butterfly spread its beautiful wings to fly out the restaurant's door and up into the sky. Up, up, up, and up toward the sun it flew, never looking back. Because at that precise moment, one of the seagulls nesting along the bank of the Hobohemian side of the Hudson River swooped from the sky, snapped up Just Jeff with its beak, and swallowed the caterpillar, human, butterfly, her new friend, in one bite. Thus, the only words the woman had left to utter were, "*Bye-bye, slatki leptire, bye-bye*." So, if you spoke Croatian or were not too lazy to translate it with an online Google translator, you'd know she was saying, "Bye-bye, sweet butterfly, bye-bye."

Maybe not today, and it may not even be tomorrow, but perhaps sometime in the future, the yet-to-be-invented innovation will be invented that will completely protect caterpillars, humans, butterflies, and even Alice and all her friends. But I'm sorry to be the one to say, sadly, that day just wasn't today...

***Bye-bye,***
***slatki leptire,***
***bye-bye.***

# Chapter IX

## Queen for a Day

It could've been because her mind was so muddled with all the insane distractions and diversions occurring. Or, how time was moving backward, along with all the curious characters of recent acquaintance, but Alice was now aware; it was later than she thought. The crazy clock above the bar read precisely 5:03 PM (and it was a very, very, very well-read clock at that, but let's discuss that more at another time, shall we?). Perchance it was merely to take her mind off these things. So, she dervishly dove into her work in and around the restaurant.

One of The Hatter's patrons, in particular, caught her eye. That would be a woman sitting in one of the back booths, adorned from head to toe in white. It wasn't so much the outfit as it was what she wore upon her head; a beautifully bedazzling, gem-studded crown! It was also because she was trying to catch Alice's attention and was now staring at the waitress while moving her hands about in the air. The woman in white was scribbling on her palm, employing pantomime to convey the universally accepted and understood gesture used between customers and waitstaff as a wordless way of saying; check, please.

As any competent member of any basic eatery establishment would do, the client's bill was tallied, totaled, carried to the crowned customer ensconced in an MHR&B faux-leather billfold, and left on the table to be paid.

"Here you go, ma'am."

"Yes, you may now call me madam, no longer the need to continue addressing me as your majesty."

"I beg your pardon, madam?"

"Oh, are you not, or I guess I should learn to say, were you not one of my subjects?"

"One of your subjects, madam? I'm not sure if I understand what you mean. Actually, I feel as if there's not anything I truly understand any longer."

"Yes, one of my, or was one of my, loyal subjects."

"I'm no one's subject, madam."

"Well, that could certainly be a subject left to debate. What is your name, dear?"

"It's Alice, your majesty… I mean madam."

"Well, Alice, being queen is not everything it's made out to be. Don't believe the hype! To begin with, it's very lonely at the top. Nearly impossible to find anyone you may truly trust or confide in."

"Oh, I know that feeling, madam. I mean the trusting and confiding part."

"Then there are all the sycophants, who pretend to be your

friends but would just as soon stab you in the back for their gain as look at you."

"That does sound royally dreadful, madam."

"Oh, it is, and don't get me started on this crown!" her majesty, we mean the lady in white, told her server as she began lifting it from her head, but first, had to ask said server for some assistance untangling the hair which had become entangled. Once Alice had succeeded in helping her with the coronet-tangled hair, the woman sat the heavenly headwear beside her on the bench of the booth where she was seated, to continue their conversation.

"Alice, it is Alice, right? Good! And, about the crown, I mean, the weight of it alone is nearly enough to crush one's soul. Now that's something they never tell you about in queen school."

"You went to queen school, madam?"

"Well, truth be told, I was only enrolled for a semester or so at some community college when this knight who rescued me from some pissy little dragon turned out to be a prince. Then I had no other choice but to marry the moron. Really, what else could one do but drop out of queen school, wed the dolt, hang around long enough until he'd become king so they could coronate me queen, and then wait for him to die, which he just did, finally, today."

"Oh my goodness, please accept my condolences for your

loss, madam. I'm very, very, very sorry. And by any chance, your rescuer wasn't the kind of knight that goes around kicking people in the bum, was he?"

"No need for you to be sorry, even if you had been the one who'd killed him. Which, of course, I know you couldn't be. Oh, by my handmaid's tail, the tail my late husband could never keep his grabby, feely mitts off of. I tried to warn King William not to ride to battle in front of his troops but to instead hide behind them, or simply stay home in the cozy castle we shared (separate bedrooms, mind you!). Oh no, Billy, don't be a hero, don't be a fool with your life, I told him. But the last thing he'd listen to, both figuratively and literally, was me. No one ever listens to little ol' *moi*. You do speak French, don't you, Alice?"

"My native tongue is Croatian. Other than that, I'm sorry to say English is the only other language I've ever learned."

"No need to be sorry again, dearest. Hearing that you don't is actually a relief. For a moment, I was afraid you were going to begin babbling back to me in French and I'd have to pretend to understand what you were saying. The only word I know in French is *moi*, and only picked that itsy bitsy *bon mot* up during one of those undergraduate semesters of queen school.

"I oftentimes wonder, even if I had completed the course, whether the tuition merited what I was taught. Between you, me, and the dungeon wall, girlfriend, if I hadn't hitched my star to some dude who'd eventually become king, I'd probably still be paying off student loans to this very day. It's a disgrace the interest rates they charge a kid trying to get a decent education. Why, oh why, didn't I just stick with the original major I'd chosen to earn my degree? Instead, I bent beneath the pressure from my parents to switch during mid-semester, and then ended up having to take useless courses like Queening 101."

"What did you want to do instead of being a queen?"

"I wanted to be a poet. But you know how parents can behave when one of their kids wants to go into the arts."

Even though Alice was unable to check the time from where she stood, she had a feeling that a significant amount of it had already lapsed in the course of this mind-boggling conversation. So, she did what any trained waitress would do to end any overly long customer contact encounter by saying, "May I get you anything else?"

"I'd like to pay you in cash, but I only have very, very, very large bills on my person, darling. But worry not; I will still leave you with a very generous tip for your troubles."

"I could always just bring you your change, madam,"

"No, I don't believe you could really bring change. Do you know why my humble servant? No? Then I must tell you. You see, true change may only come from within, which is reason number one. Reason number two is that it's always best to have no change between friends, and you have become a dear, dear, dear friend, Alice. And last but not least, they never give us queens any petty cash for spending, only credit cards. That must be a blessing for royal accountants, but it's a pain in the *derrière* for royalty."

The patron eyeballed her check and then handed over a Black American Express Centurion® card. A short time later, Alice returned with onionskin thin pieces of paper to be signed by the credit cardholder. It showed the food and beverage total, sales tax, a line to enter a gratuity amount, then a line below where the signer should add up, and then enter the total of the aforementioned sums. Before she signed the line on the front side that began with the word Signature, she read out loud, and to no one in particular, the statement that always appears between the sum total and signature lines.

"Cardmember acknowledges receipt of goods and/or services in the amount shown hereon and agrees to perform the obligations set forth by cardmember's agreement with the issuer. Ha, right, well, good luck with that, Bucko!" After which, she rapidly wrote something on the back of the vendor copy before her waitress had retrieved it.

The lady must've departed the eatery while Alice was in the kitchen picking up another order to be served to someone else. By the time the Madd Hatter employee returned to collect the payment, the woman was already gone. Picking up the billfold bearing the payment, she was about to walk away with it when something that was sitting upon the overstuffed faux-leather booth bench glittered and caught her eye. It was the woman in white's lovely, bejeweled crown! Alice snatched it up and then ran to the street side exit of the restaurant. Peering from the doorway, first to the right, then left, up and down the street outside, the lady was nowhere to be seen.

Returning with the faux-leather billfold in one hand and the gloriously gorgeous crown in the other, the server moved to an area where they kept the credit/debit card processing terminals. She thought to herself, “Perhaps there's some information on this receipt that would help me to return this to its rightful owner,” as she set the crown upon the bar while inspecting the bill of fare.

Immediately, two things caught her eye: 1) The name the woman had signed; The White Queen 2) In the location where patrons could include the gratuity, all she saw, in all uppercase block letters, was; ALWAYS SEE THE OTHER SIDE. So, Alice looked at the other side. In artfully scripted handwriting that possessed such a lofty degree of painstaking penmanship and breathtaking beauty that anyone would be wooed by its wonder, there were cryptic couplets written in tiny letters.

Alice, my tips for you are twofold

Now here is number ONE

We have no guarantee in life

Of one more rising sun

I've traveled all around this world

Seeing all that could be seen

Now I see so clearly

I'm truly sick of being Queen

So, take my crown and wear it

Even if only for this day

But please be sure to share it

Before you go away

When you meet the pauper

Give freely from your heart

For all must come to an end

For your final life to start

Within your time do what you can

To soothe the pain of strife

With kindness care for others

Do good always with your life

When we go and how we go

Answers not the question why

All we take in our departing

Is just this life, when we die

Tip TWO applies solely to you

Before you come undone

Depend not on tomorrow

Some tomorrows never come

Live every hour like your last

Because you never knew

Life went faster than you planned

When the mirror you went through

Below the poem was this note: With kind regards, and please do good always,

Pam the Poet (formerly known as The White Queen)

PS: Please keep the crown— if only for less than a day— I'm so sick of what it always does to my hair)

What was this cryptic ciphering about on the back of The White Queen's credit card receipt? Alice so wished Naida/Dinah, the White Rabbit, Just Jeff, or almost anyone else with a friendly face were still around and available to her so she could seek some sum of conference and consultation. Since they were not, she rested the crown atop her head while she read the poem for a second time. But even after the second reading, followed by a third, and finally a fourth, its meaning still eluded her…

***Some tomorrows never come***

# Chapter X

## *Whole Lotta Shakin' Going On!*

Alice was still wearing the crown when she became aware of a scuffle at the door. One of the bouncers was in some sort of an altercation there. As she neared to see and hear what was going on, the following event played out.

“Mister, I have money enough to pay for my food. Please let me in like any other person,” said a disheveled and somewhat unkempt-looking woman wearing a heavy winter overcoat though the day was hot and even a bit sticky from the dense humidity that permeated the now stuffy and steamy air. From her shoulder hung a bag with what appeared to be an assortment of equally dirty and soiled stuffed animals. “I have the money, mister, see? Please have half a heart, sir.”

Holding out a handful of change in her palm so the bouncer would see she wasn’t lying, the woman hoped against all hope that he’d find it in his heart to let her in. Alice was now standing next to the two of them. Without warning or provocation, the bouncer muttered a curse beneath his breath and heartlessly smacked all the coins from her outstretched hand. The money went spilling inside the door and all across the MHB&R floor. Grabbing her roughly by the shoulders, he pushed her further out the door and into the direction of the street.

“Jude!” she screeched at the top of her lungs, “Stop it, just stop it, I, I, I know her. She’s a friend of mine,” Alice lied. “Get away from her, I'll take care of this.

Whether it was the tone and strength of her voice or the enraged and berserk burning look of her eyes, the bouncer wordlessly retreated and left them alone. The broken and dejected woman, who appeared to be homeless and more than a little down on her luck, had already begun to despairingly walk away.

"Ma'am, please wait. I want to help you."

Slowly, with caution and trepidation, the woman turned to ask, "You want to help me, dear?" and then moved back, but not through, the doorway which she dared not enter again.

"I have to help. Maybe it's the last thing I'll ever truly and fully understand. You see, I do now know if you possess the ability to help someone in need, then just pretend they're not there and do nothing, you've committed a sin equally egregious as all the others detailed in the Bible's Ten Commandments. I know it's not explained exactly that way anywhere in the Good Book, and I haven't read all of it, but enough of it to know it's a message they're trying to tell us on every page; be kind to one another—do good always! Eight words, eight little words, and if we only all lived by those words, then what a wonderful world this would be. Wait a minute, ma'am, please just wait a minute. I have to help."

Going down on her hands and knees before the stranger, and with head hung so humbly low that one would've thought the crown Alice wore could've slipped and fallen off, she crawled about collecting the coins. When the last was retrieved, she stood before the waiting woman; counting them to be sure all had been recovered. In total, they numbered thirteen. Funny, when Alice had first begun gathering, she was sure they were nickels, dimes, or quarters. Now, tallying them up, there seemed to be—oh my!—they appeared to be thirteen pieces of silver!

"I found thirteen, ma'am. If there are more to find, please tell me and I'll search again."

Even though the destitute woman's lips looked cracked and sore, and there were many teeth missing, when she smiled in confirmation of the number, it was the most beatific smile Alice had ever had the privilege to accept.

"Yes, Alice, thirteen right on the nose. Those pieces of silver, as well as another incident eons past that weighs upon my heart and soul, were mine to bear for as long as I remember. And I'll probably continue carrying them through eternity. I once did something that I'm not proud of, to someone who loved me with all their heart and soul. In a way, they're like my cross to bear. I'll be on my way now, dear."

"Wait, please wait!" she beseeched the woman who had not yet turned to depart. Lifting the crown away and up from her noodle, Alice placed it upon the other woman's head and said, "I must give you this. I want you to have it, ma'am."

"What, you want me to have what may be one of your most prized possessions? You're willing to apportion and give your crown to a pauper, Alice?"

Placing a hand over her heart prior to saying another word, she knew that although well-intentioned, the words which the pauper had just spoken could no longer be held as true. Or at least they were no longer Alice's truth. "No, it's not what I value most anymore, ma'am."

"Then you do indeed have a very kind and noble spirit, girl, and I bless you," she said while walking away from The Hatter, crowned in all her glory. As Alice watched her leave, a hand was still above her heart—and with a start—she realized—it was no longer beating.

What was that?!?! The entire building of which The Madd Hatter Bar & Restaurant was a part, now shook with a tremor and a rumble for several seconds before stopping. Was it an earthquake? Alice wasn't sure if Hobohemia had ever been hit by one before. She knew for certain during the time she'd made the trip on her electric scooter between Brooklyn and the restaurant she could not recall ever hearing of this sort of occurrence in the past.

To be absolutely honest, since her head had been hurting for whatever reason, it was increasingly difficult to sift through thoughts, as well as clearly recall past memories. Like what had happened prior to the last nearly 24 hours, or where she'd parked the Segway and left her protective headgear. How had she come by that nasty bump on her forehead that ceaselessly throbbed and perhaps bled a bit?

Once more, the entire structure vibrated as it was struck by these odd, sudden shock waves from somewhere unknown. What was even odder, no one else within the walls of the MHR&B took notice of the occurrence, only Alice. Just as peculiar, nothing had fallen from any shelves or cabinets. The beer mugs hanging from hooks that held them suspended above the bartender's side of the bar neither swayed nor moved. The seismic phenomena that Alice had first noted occurring at 1:07 PM, (at least according to the time-warped Hatter timepiece) showed no sign of relenting.

Again and again, it felt as if the building was rocking and shaking and rattling and rolling uncontrollably. Meanwhile, for most, life within those walls went on in a much-blinded bliss of ignorance. No one around her seemed to be aware, much less than show any sign of concern or panic. "*Što nije u redu s ovim ljudima? Svi ili spavaju ili im mozak ne radi!*" Alice thought to herself. Oh, and which was Croatian, of course, for "What's wrong with these people? They all must be either asleep or brain dead!"

Each wave of the increasingly violent tremors shook her to the bone and rattled her brain. It was even becoming difficult to maintain balance as they continued ceaselessly. As a precaution, she reached backwar and latched onto the edge of the bar behind;

worrying her legs would go weak and buckle.

"Doesn't anyone else feel that?" Alice now screamed at them. "What's wrong with you people? Why are you all just sitting there doing nothing like a bunch of brain-dead zombies?"

Nary a one had raised their head to acknowledge her cries. Nay, none halted conversations nor pulled cell phones out to call for help or to say a final farewell to loved ones they'd never see again. All were oblivious to what was happening. What's wrong with them? What was wrong with all of them? What, in all of God's great glory as She watched over them, was the hell wrong with everyone?

Then, like a sun rising on a brand-new day, it dawned on Alice. No one had heard her. She screamed louder and louder and louder, but to no avail. They all just went on drinking and talking. Going about their business as if she wasn't even in the same world, or dimension, much less than the same bar, as them! She must somehow, someway, and not later but now, get them to hear her. It was a monumental matter of life and death, after all.

Spotting Frottage Frank in a corner, leaning in far too much while he spoke to one of the other waitresses, she made her way while teetering on unsteady legs toward him and hollered, "Frank, Frank, don't you feel it? That shaking, those tremors, the quaking and the shuddering; don't you feel anything at all?"

But Frank, now with his hand on the cornered waitress's curvaceous hip, displayed not a sign he'd felt anything unusual or had heard her shouting at him. He just went on talking while the trapped woman with him attempted to squirm away and out of the touchy-feely creep's reach.

Alice, from the corner of her eye, saw the Jabberwocky had emerged from the laird he employed as his office and was walking the length of the barroom, calmly and without a care. Running to him, she implored, "We have to get these people out of here before the whole building collapses. And we have to do it right this moment. It's getting worse! It's getting worse! It's getting so, so, so very much worse now!"

Although for a moment, a concerned look had spread across the Jabberwocky's beard stubble face. He immediately stuck a stubby finger in the air in a gesture of *fiat lux*, as if he'd remembered something, and then walked back in the direction of the office he'd exited, as though not seeing her.

Thinking that this was a joke that everyone was in on but her, from all the employees to a few of the regulars, she now sought the assistance of strangers. Table by table, person by person, the weary and worried woman, without success, did all within her weakening power to make them hear, see, acknowledge, and confirm her existence in some fashion. But not a single soul appeared to have heard, seen, acknowledged, or could confirm that

Alice was even alive!

The trembling and the shaking were so severe she now decided if they didn't want to be saved from certain death, and then she had no other choice than to save herself. In a state of complete, abject, hopeless horror, Alice did her best to cross the length of the uneven barroom floor to make it out and through the door. Her feet felt leaden, becoming ever heavier with each step she took in that direction.

"You're all going to die if you don't get out right now!" she shrieked as she ran. "Get out, get out, get out, before the building collapses on you and you're buried in a grave of rubble. Get your sorry asses out before it's too late!" Since no one would listen to her, what other choice had she but to leave them all behind.

As if in a dream, Alice moved in slow-motion that decreased in velocity the nearer she came to her desired destination of making it out the door. Had gravity been turned up one increment above ten, its uppermost level, and was now set at eleven? Staring above at the ceiling, for some inexplicable reason, it appeared to be the undercarriage of a motor vehicle. Hopefully, the nauseating dizziness she felt in the pit of her stomach couldn't get much worse than it was—but it did—and would simply not diminish.

The whole room spun about like one of those stupid carnival rides. The kind that by the time it stopped, you were ready to puke your guts out along with all the cotton candy, popcorn, sickly sweet drinks, corn dogs, and any other crappy carnival cuisine consumed while visiting an amusement park. And there was nothing to think of that was amusing about what was now happening to Alice. Her skin had grown cold and clammy as red-hot bolts of fire shot through her tired body in flashes. Her legs turning to rubber, the spine she needed for support melting like a Popsicle left out in the sun, and legs buckling beneath her.

With a sad sigh of recognition and resignation of what was happening, the floor suddenly rushed upwards to meet her downward falling face. She landed upon it head first, collapsing unconscious and still inside The Madd Hatter Bar & Restaurant. A mere eight feet away from the door through which Alice had sought salvation…

*...willing*
*to apportion*
*and give*
*your crown*
*to a*
*pauper...*

# Chapter XI

## Hello Darkness, My Old Friend

It was so, so, so, dark; cold, and scary too. No light, no feeling, no sound, and no idea where she was or what had happened. No, wait a minute—there was a sound—a really, really, really faint sound.

"Alice? Alice? Can you hear me now, Alice?"

It was a voice from the darkness, a very, very, very kind, gentle, and understanding voice. Without a doubt, it belonged to a woman. A voice Alice was sure she'd heard before. Once, in Croatia one night as she knelt before her small child-size bed, saying her prayers when she was only four or five years old. The second time was at The Madd Hatter Bar & Restaurant, it was either the woman dressed in white who had left her a poem, or perhaps the pauper she'd crowned.

"Alice, don't be frightened. What happened to you has, or will happen to everyone, eventually. Alice, can you hear me?"

Her eyes, now fluttering like some egret lifting above a lagoon to fly up and away, struggled to open fully. Concentrating intensely, she fought to regain consciousness, doing her best to identify the speaker.

"That's alright, Alice; take a second to come out of it entirely. That trip from there to here always takes a lot out of the soul. Just ask my Son sometime, and that boy will give you quite an earful of what happened to him when he made the trip.

"I told him not to go, but you know the way kids are and how they never listen to a parent. I tried to tell him they wouldn't understand why he was there, and he'd only freak them out. That it was way, way, way too soon yet, and they still needed more time to evolve to a point where they could love one another more than they loved themselves. But that boy! I mean, he has a good heart, and he was all hell-bent on saving them. There are times I suspect my Son suffers from a messiah complex or something. I mean the way he cares about helping those in need and all. Well, I guess that's his cross to bear. But no one ever listens to little ol' *moi*!

"If you're feeling up to it now, Alice, and would like to talk, I'm sure you have questions I'd be happy to help with, as well as a few things to tell you."

With the assistance of the woman speaking, she struggled to sit up. Studying the surroundings, nothing seemed familiar. "Where am I?"

"You're here now, but you may also be wherever you want, whenever you like, you are now part of The One. Therefore, you are everywhere."

"Am I dead?"

"We don't use that term. For, as you'll learn from being here with us, death does not exist in the sense that people are accustomed to defining it. Alice, nothing that has lived has ever truly died—the truth is—everything simply changes—then continues to go on infinitely."

"But I don't understand!"

"I do. There's much to know and understand, but you have all the time now that there ever was. So just lay back again, close your eyes, and dream of where you really want to be."

"May I first ask you something else?"

"Of course, my dear friend, it's so rare anyone really listens to what little ol' *moi* has to say, so it'd be a pleasure," God told her.

"My baby, is my baby, okay? Did my baby make it?"

Giving Alice's hand a motherly and supportive squeeze, she whispered, "Close your eyes, Alice, and go to sleep now. Dream of where you want to be and who you want to be with you, and if that's your daughter, then she will be there. I promise you."

Laying her head back down on the pillow that was soft as a cottony cloud, Alice closed her eyes, wondering what her daughter would look like, as the young woman slipped into a deep, deep, deep sleep. Lost in this slumber, she was home, back in her native land of Croatia, in the city of Zagreb, far from the country's broken coastline along the Adriatic Sea. And somewhere, far, far, far, but not so far away it was out of earshot, she heard a tiny baby cry…

***Am***

***I***

***dead?***

HELODALI
DALI'S GLASS

# Chapter XII

## Where's My Happily Ever After?

When the late-night accident occurred, there was no one else on the street. After the electric scooter had struck the side of the small truck festooned with unframed sheets of glass and mirrors along its side, and she went headlong and helmet first over the handlebars and through a looking glass, another interesting phenomenon of physics had occurred. Going over those handlebars, both feet had reflexively locked around the steering column in a failed attempt of saving herself. That in and of itself was not the interesting phenomenon of physics which an earlier reference was already made. Due to the vehicle's velocity and the angle of impact, the 26+ lbs, foldable Segway ES2 scooter slid sideways and beneath the parked van. With Alice's feet being locked in the way they were, it had dragged her body as it slid beneath the carrier and out of view, along with itself.

For many hours she lay unconscious, hurt, and bleeding beneath the undercarriage. As night became early morning, a pedestrian or two, several cars, and a lone jogger had passed by without seeing her. It wasn't until an observant member of the Hobohemian Police Department first noticed the broken glass and mirror, then later what was determined to be chunks of chrome, some other metal bits strewn on the street and beneath the rig, as well as a cell phone, two CDs still shrink-wrapped in jewel cases, and what appeared to be an enveloped card. Upon closer inspection, the officer noticed a single skid mark by the van.

Peering beneath, he saw what any person on the force of Hobohemia's finest dreaded most to see.

"This is unit eight. This is unit eight. I have what appears to be a female beneath a vehicle severely injured and bleeding. Send an ambulance and request backup. Send ambulance and backup ASAP. This is an emergency, repeating this is an emergency, over and out!"

By the time most folks were on their way to work that day, the ambulance had already arrived. With the help of two cops, the two EMS workers were able to remove Alice's body from underneath the truck where it had been trapped. After a quick examination, the more medically proficient of the emergency team had determined the girl was still alive, but just barely. He reported to the commanding officer at the scene that evidence indicated she'd been there for several hours, unconscious and losing blood, and her prognosis was far from good.

Again, with the EMS and the HPD working shoulder to shoulder, they managed to slip a support slat under Alice's limp, bruised, and bleeding body, in case of any spinal injuries. The responders then got her up on a collapsible gurney, and with sirens blaring, whisked the woman off to the closest hospital emergency room. After a few blocks, the attendant who was riding in the back shouted to the driver, "You can slow down and turn the siren off. I'm calling this. She's gone. The time of death is 9:01 AM. Let's take the body in and then grab some coffee."

And with that, our tale comes to a close. Or does it…

*This is unit eight.*
*This is unit eight.*

# The End

Or is it…

FINIS?

# Epilogue

This was it! And Buckley felt just like turning around and going home without playing the song he wanted her to hear. The one he'd written for her on the subject of a potential "them." His mouth couldn't have gotten any drier than if it were stuffed full of super-absorbent, super-jumbo Berkley Jensen organic cotton balls. Right now he felt like an out-of-place idiot standing in the middle of a busy bar/restaurant with his guitar strapped uncomfortably to his right shoulder. Instead, he decided to stay and just give it his best shot.

An entertainer The Madd Hatter Bar & Restaurant had hired to perform for the night just announced he'd be taking a short break. So, the house DJ filled the momentary silence with songs that only a younger crowd probably knew a line or two of the lyrics well enough to sing along with, here and there. Halfway between the make-shift stage and the men's restroom, Buckley was able to intercept the exiting performer and offer his deal.

"Hey!"

"Hey!"

"First off, solid set, man. Well played! Now second, let's make a deal."

"What kind of fucking deal are we fucking talking about here?"

"You clear it with the manager here, and if you guys let me

play just one song, I'll give you $100 in cash."

Buckley knew talk was cheap, so he held out the C-note as a testimonial to his sincerity and integrity. This offering, an act accepted without delay by the other party in the transaction, was a small price to pay if he could only get her to hear what he had poured his heart into and composed. He'd come prepared; so, if the performer had wanted more than the original offer tendered, Buckley had some wiggle room stashed in the wallet nestled in the back pocket of his blue jeans. But now, the deal was done—and at a bargain-basement price to boot!

"Remember, you have to clear it with the manager here. I don't want to get shut down less than a minute into it after giving you $100. Deal?"

"Deal—but I don't need to clear it with no fucking manager. That's my fucking equipment. This is my fucking show. If the fucking manager here has any fucking problem with it, he can fucking take it up with fucking me. I'll punch his fucking lights out like I fucking did last week. Now I've got to drop a few fucking kids off for a fucking swimming lesson, so you just go and play for as fucking long as you fucking like."

Catching the house DJ's eye, then making a slashing motion at his throat to give him the "fucking cut-it!" sign, the bowel movement challenged performer then disappeared into the men's room to keep the aforementioned swim class appointment.

Following the orders of the only one who appeared to be in fucking charge here, the house music abruptly cut out, and a terrifying shock of silence fell upon the establishment.

Buckley marched with resolution in the direction of the make-shift stage. Upon it were; two microphones on stands, a speaker case with an amp head resting on top where the mic-cables were attached, and a single, solitary barstool. Buckley froze—did he really want to do this—take the risk of looking like a fool in front of not only strangers but the one for whom he'd written the song, and at the restaurant where she worked waiting tables? Partially, by the forfeiting of a Benjamin, but mainly by how much he needed her to hear his song, he mustered the courage to set foot upon the small stage.

While he hadn't spotted Alice on his way into The Madd Hatter Bar & Restaurant, or even en route to the stage, he knew she must be around somewhere. Not only could Buckley sense her presence somewhere within the restaurant, but he'd also stopped by the place last night before her shift had ended, and they had spoken briefly. In all honesty, he hadn't innocently just dropped in for a drink last night; Naida, not only another Madd Hatter server but Alice's friend, had tipped him off during a prior visit that the object of his affection would be celebrating her twenty-sixth birthday yesterday. So, Buckley had come bearing gifts.

A while ago, Alice, who was born in Croatia, had shared

with him who her favorite recording artists were. One was a female rapper from Slovenia called Senidah (aka The Balkan Trap Diva). The other, a Bosnian singer-songwriter, was Dino Merlin (aka The Wizard). So, doing his due diligence Buckley logged into his Amazon Prime account to find and purchase a CD by each of them. From a bit of research on Wikipedia, he discovered that the Slovenian's most notable hit record was "*Slađana*" and that Merlin's was "*Ruža.*" Buckley made sure he'd bought an album from each on which they were included.

In addition, he'd also picked up a simple birthday card for her and written a message that said, "Alice—happy b'day! Hope you still have a CD player at your place, and if not, I'll be happy to rip the tracks and send them to you. Best b'day wishes—Buckley." He'd toyed with the thought of signing it, "Love, Buckley'" but was worried it might be slightly overplaying his hand. After all, the lovelorn lad was still not quite sure where he stood with the desired red-haired woman of his dreams.

When he'd been there last night to drop off his gift he stayed long enough for a beer before giving her the CDs and card. When paying for the drink, Buckley casually asked, "You working here tomorrow?"

"Yeah, got to pay the rent, right?"

"Right."

"Buckley, I'm pregnant."

To say this took him by surprise was an understatement. Regaining composure, he replied, "Then we should talk."

"Not now. It's my birthday and I just found out the staff is throwing a little party to celebrate after we close. Besides, I'm slammed with tables tonight. And yes, we should talk. Can you come by tomorrow, Buckley?"

"Okay."

Standing to leave, and while fishing the gifts from his shoulder bag, the bashful boy hurriedly told her, "Happy birthday. I gotta go, but I promise I'll be back tomorrow," before rushing out of The Hatter. Feeling like he'd made a fool of himself again, Buckley went home, having not spoken the words he'd wished he'd had the courage to share with her. Once inside the tiny Hobohemian one-bedroom apartment, he picked up his steel string guitar to write her a song. The words that poured from his heart as he sang were the exact words he'd wanted to tell her from almost the first day they'd met. In about an hour, the song was written.

When the negative charge

Meets the positive charge

And they come together

The air's electrified

Ah, ah, ah Alice

Come on out tonight

Oh, oh, oh Alice

Come out to play

Let down your long red hair

Someday somewhere somebody will care

Love your beauty love all your flaws

Love pick you up every time you fall

Ah, ah, ah Alice

Come on out tonight

Oh, oh, oh Alice

Come out to play

Someone, who'll never get tired of you,

Someone, so inspired by you

Who loves everything you do

Got'em forever desiring you

Ah, ah, ah Alice

Come on out tonight

Oh, oh, oh Alice

Come out to play

Aphrodite, she envies you

Jealous of all that you do

Dance like the sea in naked moonlight

Alice, you gotta come out tonight

Ah, ah, ah Alice

Come on out tonight

Oh, oh, oh Alice

Come out to play

Alice, hold on to your life

You got to put up a fight

Live for today, play in the sun

Some tomorrows just never come

Ah, ah, ah Alice

Come on out tonight

Oh, oh, oh Alice

Come out and play

(https://youtu.be/5YRsfZEOcqU)

After composing it, he knew what his next steps had to be; return to The Madd Hatter Bar & Restaurant tomorrow night; let Alice hear his song; discuss what they needed to talk about.

Buckley set about unpacking and tuning his guitar and then checking to be sure that both microphones were live. He climbed atop the barstool on stage and launched into the tune aptly titled "Alice." Wherever she was tonight, he was sure after hearing her own name repeated while he performed, she would emerge to listen more closely. But the woman never appeared. Instead, and en route to repeating the ending chorus, he was cut off by a girl's scream.

Stopping the performance and turning around, he discovered it was Naida. With a cell phone still held to the side of her face, she began crying as she repeated a single word over and over and over again, "No! No! No! No! No! No! No! Nooooooo..."

The other waitresses from the MHB&R, all except Alice, that is, rushed to her side. Seeing that Naida had begun to swoon, one of the girls grabbed the phone while another two helped to gently ease her into a prone position on the barroom floor where she was now sobbing uncontrollably. The one with Naida's phone spoke into it, listened, and then she too began to cry. The waitress with the phone said something to the others that Buckley could not hear, like chain lightning, and in rapid succession, each turned on the waterworks.

"I can't believe it! She's…" one wailed.

Another one, "Oh my God! Oh my God! Oh my …"

In confusion, along with an unexplainable sense of dread, Buckley hopped off the barstool with the guitar still in hand and moved toward them to investigate…

Perhaps to be continued…

*Ah, ah, ah Alice*
*Come on out tonight*
*Oh, oh, oh Alice*
*Come out to play*

# Timeline of Important Events

**An unspecified time on the night of Alice's 26th birthday**: The Madd Hatter Bar & Restaurant staff throws her a surprise "tea party" after work. She felt less than celebratory as she ruminates about being stuck waiting tables, deep in debt, tired as hell, still single, all alone, and dealing with an unplanned pregnancy. Discovering The Jabberwocky (her night manager) scheduled a double shift for her to work tomorrow, Alice leaves the party early. Her destination is to return to the overpriced apartment she rents in Brooklyn, New York.

**3:15 AM**: The precise moment when Alice began to suspect that time was moving backward. Perhaps a premonition of what was yet to come? It also marks the approximate time she walks out of The Madd Hatter Bar & Restaurant, steps upon *Crvena Plesačica* (aka The Red Dancer), her Segway ES2 electric scooter, and heads down Washington Street (Hobohemia's main drag) to set a course toward her home in Brooklyn.

**3:22 AM**: The exact minute on Washington Street when Alice's Segway ES2 electric scooter hits one of Hobohemia's legendary potholes. Losing control of the vehicle, she ends up on a blind date with the side of a van festooned with unframed mirrors and glass.

**<u>3:23 AM</u>**: Alice then has a really rough one-night stand with the undercarriage and the parked van. Will the two of them end up falling headlong and over the handlebars in love?

**<u>9:01 AM</u>**: Regaining consciousness, she's aware of being back at the bar, standing before the gothic-looking clock, and now sure the timepiece's hands are headed backward in the counterclockwise direction. The only other person there is her friend and co-worker, Naida, who, as Alice notes, has already begun a steady process of transmogrification. The co-worker's friend has just finished decorating the inside of The Madd Hatter Bar & Restaurant with colorful *papier-mâché* flowers. Along with Alice, she is also one of the prank-playing Russian Doll "sisters."

**<u>8:55 AM</u>**: The two women chat for several minutes as Naida tells her "sis" she now prefers to be called Dinah. Alice beats around the bush a bit, but at 8:55 AM, she musters the courage to come right out and ask her friend if she's turning into a cat.

**<u>8:54 AM</u>**: As the two Russian Doll "sisters" continue to discuss the mysterious mouser makeover, they're rudely interrupted by Rose, a *papier-mâché* faux flower with a thorny personality. Rose offers an apology, and then Daisy, Tiger-lily, Sweet Pea, Violet, Azalea Begonia, Chrysanthemum, Dahlia, and all the other freaky *papier-mâché* flowers introduce themselves to the two waitresses.

**<u>6:53 AM</u>**: For nearly two hours, the *papier-mâché* fussy flowers babble on while Alice listens. Dinah is bored to tears by their mindless chatter, so she becomes a tad tired and nods off for a short catnap.

**<u>6:21 AM</u>**: Dinah momentarily awakens from a nightmare in which she's being chased by mice who turn into outlandishly large insects. As with Alice and the *papier-mâché* flowers, the insects make amends, and after a few hours, the dreamer and those dreamt part as friends.

**<u>2:42 AM</u>**: The Jabberwocky is interviewing Dee and Dom, a potential pair of new workers for the restaurant. Because every time he asks, "Are you experienced…', he's interrupted by raucous riffs played by The Jimi Hendrix Experience before he can complete the sentence, the interview goes nowhere and deteriorates into an impromptu poetry-slam. With every minute passing, Dinah/Naida has more cat characteristics and fewer human traits. Meanwhile, the mirror solves a mystery, Alice's head hurts, and she now finds a kind of gnarly knot has risen on her forehead—you know—the kind of lump that may arise after a nasty knock on the noggin.

**2:28 AM**: After listening outside the Jabberwocky's office door to the interview gone awry for about twenty-four minutes, Alice throws herself into doing immediate tasks at hand around the eatery.

**11:53 PM**: The Madd Hatter and his wife, The Redd Queen, owners of the MHB&R, enter. He's verbally abusive to his workers, and his wife threatens them with violence. He's apparently telepathic and is thus able to read everyone's thoughts, albeit less than perfect. They accuse Alice of being bonkers, and not recognizing Dinah as Naida they have the cat cast out onto the street. Alice feels devastated not only by having her sanity questioned but by the shabby treatment bestowed upon the transformed tabby.

**10:34 PM**: The Madd Hatter Bar & Restaurant is now packed to the rafters with hungry and thirsty patrons. Following a good cry, Alice returns to busying and distracting herself with working. Shortly thereafter, she has a rub-in, we mean run-in, with Frottage Frank, a touchy-feely close-talking bar regular who's a poor tipper, generally gross, cheap, smelly, overly obese, annoying, and frequently has great falls off barstools when he's drunk.

**10:02 PM**: Running into another Madd Hatter Bar & Restaurant regular that everyone referred to as The Reader, since he was always reading when there, Alice notices that much like Naida/Dinah, he too has begun to transmogrify, but into a White Rabbit. The White Rabbit somewhat assuages her concern about madness, as well as explains why he's always reading.

**9:44 PM**: After sharing some heartfelt advice and a few astute observations with the worried woman, The White Rabbit remembers he's late for a very important date and hops out the door.

**9:32 PM**: Alice bumps into The Jabberwocky coming out of his office. He instructs her to bring some mushrooms from the cellar up to the kitchen. In the basement, she encounters a hookah-smoking caterpillar named Just Jeff, who offers her a hit from his hookah. Whatever they've smoked leaves them hallucinating that they've grown so big they fill the entire cellar. At first, panicking, Alice regains her composure by following Just Jeff's advice to blink once, then twice. What comes next is really nice.

**9:01 PM**: Opening her eyes, she's now upstairs sitting at the bar while Just Jeff, who has now taken a human form, serves drinks from behind it. Offering her a drink, she declines. Alice, out of desperation, asks if he has any unicorns behind the bar that he'd be willing to share. Sadly, Just Jeff explains, he has no unicorn today, as the last one was eaten by a lion. Coincidentally, it also explains why we never see unicorns anymore. She then goes on a break from work.

**8:16 PM**: Returning after her break while serving her customers the drinks Just Jeff mixes, she speaks to him more. The post-happy hour crowd is still pretty thirsty, so the two work nonstop for a while. The sun has unset, and outside there's daylight.

**7:55 PM**: Alice is disturbed by having no recollection of what she's done with her Segway ES2 electric scooter. And the headaches have only worsened.

**7:43 PM**: It's then a knight attired in a full suit of armor enters the Hatter and begins, one by one, kicking patrons in the butt with his metal-clad foot.

**7:34 PM**: When The Kick-ass Knight plants an armored foot in the *derrière* of Giuseppe, who's known in the neighborhood as a bit of a tough guy, the booted man demands to know why. The Kick-ass Knight explains it's because he can, then offers him a further demonstration. Seeing the visor of the knight's helmet is in the open position, Giuseppe takes a swing, but not before the knight flips the visor back in place. After breaking his hand on the metal helmet face, the tough guy is taken, hurt and bleeding, to the hospital by his drinking buddies. But Giuseppe may not be the only injured party—Alice detects what may be blood—coming from the now swelling bump on her forehead.

**7:21 PM**: Prior to exiting The Madd Hatter Bar & Restaurant, the Kick-ass Knight imparts this message to our heroine, "A helmet is a very good way to protect your crown, Alice, but you can't always be sure it will save you. Not even when one is crowned as princess or queen." Baffled by its meaning, she asks Just Jeff if he has a clue as to what The Kick-ass Knight was trying to share.

**7:10 PM**: Horrified, she sees that Just Jeff has begun spinning a silken cocoon about him. He says he's about to change into something else again, but prior to doing so, he attempts to tell her what really happened on her last ride home. But before he can, the words are muffled by the newly constructed cocoon.

**6:57 PM**: Mistakenly believing that Just Jeff died, Alice is relieved when a pair of large pair of wings rends the silken cocoon. Emerging as a butterfly, Just Jeff flies out of The Madd Hatter Bar & Restaurant door. But while alighting toward the heavens, he's gobbled up and eaten by The Hungry Hobohemian Seagull before getting too far. Bye-bye, sweet butterfly, bye-bye.

**6:31 PM**: Since time is moving backward, this means that the night shift is coming to an end, and soon the day shift will begin. Alice usually gets a ninety-minute dinner break when pulling a double shift. Normally she'd be famished by this time, but for whatever reason, she now feels neither hunger nor thirst. So instead, she decides to check her cell phone to see what she's been missing in the world outside the walls of The Madd Hatter Bar & Restaurant. The only problem is, like her Segway ES2 electric scooter and crash helmet, the cell phone, too, is unaccounted for. How odd, how odd indeed!

**5:03 PM**: By the end of her dinner break, and perhaps it's the lack of food, drink, and/or cell phone access, Alice's headache has now gotten even worse. A woman wearing a dazzling crown and who is attired entirely in white has finished her meal at the MHB&R and asks for the check. During the usually normal act of social intercourse customers and servers are known to engage in while interacting, the regal woman reveals she was once a queen: The White Queen. The White Queen informs Alice she has abdicated her throne. Since her husband, King William, is now deceased, The White Queen also wishes to abandon her crown in order to return to her first love: Poetry. No longer requiring the title of The White Queen, she may now go back to using her previously abandoned pseudonymous moniker of Pam the Poet. The former royal highness lays some heavy truths on Alice's aching head about queening, change, and life in general during their conversation.

**4:51 PM**: Pam the Poet now decides she's found not only a new friend but a kindred spirit too. So, after Alice leaves the room, she signs the credit card receipt and then bequeaths her new soul sister with two gifts; a poem which she writes on the back of the card receipt, and the now no longer needed glittering crown.

**4:49 PM**: Alice returns to The White Queen/Pam the Poet's table to find the woman gone. All that remains are the receipt with the poem and the crown. She attempts to return the jewel-encrusted coronal, but to no avail; the woman in white has vanished beyond the doors of The Madd Hatter Bar & Restaurant and is in the wind. Although she reads Pam's poems several times, its meaning at present baffles the now waning woman. Even rereading it with The White Queen's crown atop her seriously throbbing head, the meaning at that moment still eludes her.

**2:24 PM**: Hearing a scuffle at The Madd Hatter Bar & Restaurant doorway, Alice investigates. There she finds Jude, the nastiest of The Madd Hatter Bar & Restaurant Bouncers, in a heated altercation with what appears to be a homeless woman. Although the woman does turn out to have the cash to pay for what she'd like to purchase, and after imploring the man to show half a heart toward her, Jude still will not allow her in. Even after showing him her money to assuage his concerns, the bouncer rudely slaps the hand holding it, and the coins fly across the floor of the MHB&R. At that point, Alice knows she must intervene. Whether it was the tone and strength of her voice or the enraged and berserk burning look in Alice's eyes, the bouncer wordlessly retreats. The homeless derelict begins to exit in defeat.

**2:14 PM**: From inside the doorway, Alice begs her to wait. Because of the kindness that was just shown, the woman pauses to hear her out. What she's told is how Alice now understands the assistance she wishes to provide for someone in need is no longer a choice; it's what she must do to be true to herself as an act of redemption.

**2:06 PM**: Lowering to hands and knees before the poor stranger, with head hung humbly low, Alice crawls about on the floor to collect the coins on her behalf.

**1:52 PM**: Before returning the money, it's discovered that instead of being nickels, dimes, or quarters, they're actually pieces of silver, exactly thirteen pieces of silver, to be precise. It is then explained that the silver pieces were earned long ago by participating in some dastardly deed and The Pauper still carries them, as well as the guilt, like a cross to bear for eternity.

**1:43 PM**: Before allowing The Pauper to depart, Alice gives her the dazzlingly bejeweled crown. Touched by the selflessness and generosity in this act of sharing something so valued with someone so obviously in need, she returns the kindness in the form of a blessing.

**1:08 PM**: The pain in Alice's head has become so intense she does all within her power not to scream out in agony. There's no denying any longer that there's something very, very, very wrong with the Croatian-born waitress.

**1:07 PM**: Everything around her now begins to shake and tremble. Fearing it's an earthquake, or something far worse, Alice tries to warn everyone to leave The Madd Hatter Bar & Restaurant before the building crumbles and falls upon them. Strangely, at first, they don't seem to hear her; and it then becomes evident they do not see her either. With pain now wracking her entire body, she uses what little time that remains to her to try to make the people hear and see the truth of what is happening, but to no avail.

**12:44 PM**: As the room spins, her skin turns cold and

clammy. Red-hot flashes of heat melt her spine like a Popsicle left in the sun and turn her limbs to rubber. Alice's legs buckle as she lets out a sad sigh of recognition and resignation as to what is happening. The suffering, finally unbearable, she crumbles face-first to The Madd Hatter Bar & Restaurant floor and loses consciousness eight feet away from the door through which she sought salvation.

**10:42 AM**: When Alice recovers consciousness, she is being cared for by a motherly woman, who, as it turns out, is God. As they chat, God explains what has happened and, cryptically, how in the end, everything will be okay. An opportunity is then provided for Alice to meet her unborn child.

**10:02 AM**: While on his morning patrol, an observant member from Unit 8 of the Hobohemian Police Department discovers Alice's broken body beneath the undercarriage of the van she'd smashed into while riding her Segway ES2 electric scooter home. Calling for backup and an ambulance, they remove her badly injured body, and she's still alive. After nearly an hour, the EMS team has her in their ambulance, with sirens blaring, and whisks the woman off to the closest hospital emergency room.

**9:01 AM**: En route, Alice succumbs to death. The attendant riding in the back with her tells the driver, "…slow down and turn the siren off. I'm calling this. She's gone. The time of death is 9:01 AM. Let's take the body in and then grab some coffee."

**9:02 AM**: Time now begins to move forward again, and perhaps, so shall we...

**7:01 PM on the evening after Alice's 26$^{th}$ birthday**: Buckley sings his song, Naida receives some news, and the waitresses turn on the waterworks.

# Poems and Songs

## Dee's Spoken Word Words

Tweedle me this then tweedle me that

Agree to tweedle and twaddle

For tweedle me this then tweedle me that

Been so bored by all your prattle

Just what you say it matters not

As you ask of our experience

Ponder this then ponder that

What makes you so f-ing curious?

## Alice's Looking-Glass Incantation

Mirror, mirror, on the wall.

Do you understand this hot mess at all?

## Dee's Spoken Words Reflected in the Looking-Glass

Tweedle me this then tweedle me that

Agree to tweedle and twaddle

For tweedle me this then tweedle me that

Been so bored by all your prattle

Just what you say it matters not

As you ask of our experience

Ponder this then ponder that

What makes you so f-ing curious?

**<u>Just Jeff/Hookah Smoking Caterpillar/Man/Butterfly's Rhyme</u>**

Just Jeff, I need no other name

For I'm not fish, or foul, nor game.

Although I'm not like other people,

I'm a person, just the same.

So please, it's Just Jeff,

For Just Jeff's my only name."

No, I'm Just Jeff, but okay,

You may have it your way

Obviously,

I'm taking a hit off this hookah.

Would you like one too?

I'm happy to share, happy to share with you.

Take a hit; take a hit,

Perhaps a hit or two?

Hold it in, hold it in,

Then let it out to do it all again.

Blink your eyes, first once, then twice.

What comes next is really, really nice.

We grew,

And grew,

And grew.

But worry not,

The growing's stopped,

Now dream of what you'd like to do.

## One of The Lady in White/The White Queen/Pam the Poet's Gift for Alice

Alice, my tips for you are twofold

Now here is number ONE

We have no guarantee in life

Of one more rising sun

I've traveled all around this world
Seeing all that could be seen
Now I see so clearly
I'm truly sick of being Queen

So, take my crown and wear it
Even if only for this day
But please be sure to share it
Before you go away

When you meet the pauper
Give freely from your heart
For all must come to an end
For your final life to start

Within your time do what you can

To soothe the pain of strife
With kindness care for others
Do good always with your life

When we go and how we go
Answers not the question why
All we take in our departing
Is just this life, when we die

Tip TWO applies solely to you
Before you come undone
Depend not on tomorrow
Some tomorrows never come

Live every hour like your last
Because you never knew
Life went faster than you planned
When the mirror you went through

**Buckley's Song for Alice**

When the negative charge

Meets the positive charge

And they come together

The air's electrified

Ah, ah, ah Alice

Come on out tonight

Oh, oh, oh Alice

Come out to play

Let down your long red hair

Someday somewhere somebody will care

Love your beauty love all your flaws

Love to pick you up every time you fall

Ah, ah, ah Alice

Come on out tonight

Oh, oh, oh Alice

Come out to play

Someone, who'll never get tired of you,

Someone, so inspired by you

Who loves everything you do

Got'em forever desiring you

Ah, ah, ah Alice

Come on out tonight

Oh, oh, oh Alice

Come out to play

Aphrodite she envy you

Jealous of all that you do

Dance like the sea in naked moonlight

Alice, you gotta come out tonight

Ah, ah, ah Alice

Come on out tonight

Oh, oh, oh Alice

Come out to play

Alice, hold on to your life

You got to put up a fight

Live for today, play in the sun

Some tomorrows just never come

Ah, ah, ah Alice

Come on out tonight

Oh, oh, oh Alice

Come out and play

# Translations

*Crvena Plesačica* (Croatian) = The Red Dancer (English)

*Da li si zaista mačka*? (Croatian) = Are you a cat? (English)

*Oh, sranje!" - Što se dovraga događa*? (Croatian) = Oh, shit! What the hell is happening? (English)

*Ne znam. Možda se zabavljaju ili nešto* (Croatian) = I don't know. Perhaps they're rocking out or something. (English)

*Je li netko pustio sovu unutra?* (Croatian) = Had someone let an owl slip into this place? (English)

*Bye-bye, slatki leptire, bye-bye.* (Croatian) = Bye-bye, sweet butterfly, bye-bye. (English)

*Što nije u redu s ovim ljudima? Svi ili spavaju im mozak ne radi!* (Croatian) = What's wrong with these people? They all must be either asleep or brain dead! (English)

*Ruža* (Croatian) = Rose(English)

# Cast

# of

# Characters

**Alice**: A Croatian immigrant working her ass off at a food and beverage establishment for minimum wage plus tips.

**An Officer from the Hobohemian Police Department**: The first to discover Alice's body after The Electric Scooter accident.

**Azalea**: One of the flowers Naida had fashioned out of *papier-mâché* and hung as decoration in The Madd Hatter Bar & Restaurant.

**Begonia**: The ever so shy *papier-mâché* flower.

**Buckley:** Someone who cares about Alice, sadly, more than she'll ever know.

**Chrysanthemum**: An overly curious *papier-mâché* flower.

**Crvena Plesačica**: Alice's Segway ES2 electric scooter (aka The Red Dancer).

**Dahlia**: Another *papier-mâché* flower.

**Daisy**: Still another *papier-mâché* flower.

**Dee**: One of the two interviewees the Jabberwocky questions about their experience during an interview at The Madd Hatter Bar & Restaurant for a job to work for minimum wage plus tips. Dee fancies herself as a bit of a poetry-slamming poet.

**Dinah**: The cat that Naida (Alice's good friend/coworker at The Madd Hatter Bar & Restaurant and who's also one-half of The Russian Doll sisters) is eventually transmogrified into becoming.

**Dom**: The second of the two interviewees the Jabberwocky questions about their experience during an interview at The Madd Hatter Bar & Restaurant for a job to work for minimum wage plus tips. Dom too also fancies herself as a poet.

**Frottage Frank**: Brother of The Redd Queen, brother-in-law of The Madd Hatter. Interestingly enough, Frank's birthday is any time he's broke and thirsty. Women have been known to label him as a close-talker who's far too touchy-feely. He's a poor tipper who was generally gross, cheap, smelly, overly obese, annoying, and known to frequently have great falls off barstools while drunk.

**God**: She who needs no introduction.

**Giuseppe**: One of The Madd Hatter Bar & Restaurant patrons who is an unfortunate recipient of The Kick-ass Knight's armored boot up the ass. Giuseppe, reputed to be a bit of a tough guy in and around the neighborhood, was not as tough as some thought he was.

**Giuseppe's Drinking Buddies**: Friends who were drinking with Giuseppe, a tough guy in and around the neighborhood, at The Madd Hatter Bar & Restaurant the night of the Kick-ass Knight assault. With their assistance after the attack, Giuseppe was taken to a hospital for emergency care. Sure hope that was something his health insurance covered!

**Hobohemia**: A fabled and mythical land somewhere in the wilds of New Jersey. It's populated by artists and Wiccans and witches and wizards and writers as well as various animals and an assortment of others. It's also the adopted home of the author of this book. World-renowned for the kindness of its inhabitants, as well as the location where the first baseball game was played between two teams, the birthplace of Frank Sinatra, and possesses more bars, pubs, restaurants, and taverns per square foot than any other city in the United States of America.

**Jimi Hendrix**: A groundbreaking musician from the 1960s who was a driving force in the creation of the acid-rock music genre that blew so many minds way back when and is still blowing minds today.

**Jude**: One of the hefty, husky Madd Hatter Bar &

Restaurant Bouncers who decide who comes in or not. Some say that Jude possesses less than half a heart. Some others have concluded it would be a vast overestimate of his true heart size. From time to time, he also acts as part of The Madd Hatter's and Redd Queen's security team. Pet peeves? Well, what'cha you got?

**Just Jeff**: An ever-evolving hookah-smoking caterpillar-man-butterfly. Just Jeff, who's a kick-ass bartender, evolves into becoming another of Alice's confidants. Jeff is also one of the few rare individuals who have figured out why we no longer encounter unicorns in this day and age.

**King William**: Recently deceased husband of the crown-cursed White Queen. If only he'd heeded his wise wife's warnings of, "...Billy, don't be a hero, don't be a fool with your life...", instead of leading his troops from the front as opposed to hiding behind them, King William may very well still have been alive today.

**Naida**: Alice's good friend and coworker at The Madd Hatter Bar & Restaurant. She's also one-half of The Russian Doll sisters.

**Pam the Poet**: A pre-coronation pseudonym used by The White Queen; the woman at The Madd Hatter Bar & Restaurant dressed completely in white and wearing a beautiful crown who Alice befriends and later leaves the waning waitress two valuable tips. An NYU Queen School dropout, who, due to parental pressure, changed her degree from English Literature to Queening. She also shares with our heroine the lack of compatibility and communication in the relationship with her recently deceased spouse, King William, and how she always just wanted to be a poet. After abdicating the throne by relinquishing the use of the title "Your Majesty," she re-embraced and resumed using her former and more humble title of Pam the Poet.

**Rose**: A blood-red *papier-mâché* flower which on occasion that is known to be a might thorny.

**Sweet Pea**: Yet another *papier-mâché* flower.

**The Baby**: Alice's unplanned, unborn child, who, as it turns out, has been endowed with a very healthy and powerful pair of lungs.

**The Beetles**: Some of the apologetic bugs chasing Dinah/Noika in a dream during a catnap.

**The Bible**: A book used far too often in contradiction of the original purpose for which it was written. Frequently employed to alienate, berate, condemn, damage, eliminate, fetter, govern, hate, so on and so forth. Wielded regularly as a weapon against those not completely and totally in agreement with someone holding it. It's sometimes utilized in subjugating the freedom of the many in order to benefit the will of only a few.

**The Crown**: A noggin topper that may bear a weighty weight on some who wear it. Believe it or not, most crowns are hand-me-downs. In this tale, it's passed down from The White Queen to Alice, who then hands it off to The Pauper. Who The Pauper next pawns it off to is never actually revealed to us. The Crown is also murder on women's hairdos—causing tangles and knots —and worse of all—split ends.

**The Dali Glass Co. Van**: The immovable object that Alice, the unstoppable force, meets in what may have been one of the worst and deadliest attempts ever to solve an age-old irresistible unstoppable force paradox when encountering immovable objects.

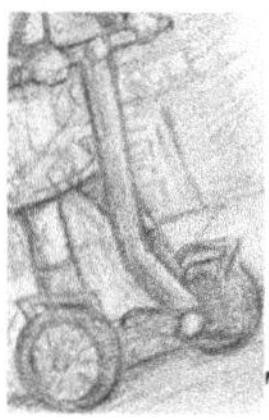

**The Electric Scooter**: Alice's second most

preferred way to roll (only surpassed by rideable unicorns—and which we all not only know no longer roam this Earth—but thanks to this book—the reason why…).

**The EMS Team:** The Hobohemian emergency medical workers who along with members of Hobohemian Police Department, help in removing Alice's broken body from under the vehicle it's been trapped and hidden beneath since her accident. The EMS Team attempts to stabilize, resuscitate, and then get the near-fatally injured woman to a hospital in time to save her life. Unfortunately, for any involved, they fail in that final effort.

**The Enormous Ephemerid**: Another apologetic bug Dinah/Naida encounters in a dream while catnapping.

**The Helmet of Protective Headgear**: The crash helmet that was worn by Alice when riding her Segway ES2 electric scooter on the trips between her high rent home in Brooklyn and her relatively low paying job at The Madd Hatter Bar & Restaurant in Hobohemia.

**The Hookah Smoking Caterpillar**: Is also

known as Jeff, or Just Jeff, a.k.a. the butterfly, a kick-ass bartender, and an Alice confidant. He's not averse to sharing his stash with a stranger, speaking in rhymes at times, or explaining the absence of mythical creatures when queried.

**The Hungry Hobohemian Seagull**: When Just Jeff said, "Alice, we don't live forever," one would never have imagined he knew his own demise would come about between the beak of The Hungry Hobohemian Seagull who lived along the banks of the Hobohemian side of the Hudson River. Nope, never saw that one a' coming...

**The Insects**: The Insects are what The Mice in Dinah's dream transformed into when The Mice were cornered.

**The Jabberwocky**: The night manager at The Madd Hatter Bar & Restaurant.

**The Jimi Hendrix Experience**: A groundbreaking power-trio from the 1960s led by Hendrix, a driving force in the creation of acid-rock. Respectfully, the surviving

bandmates never even discussed, much less considered, carrying on and replacing Jimi after his death.

**The Kick-ass Knight**: An armor-clad knight who goes around kicking people in the ass merely because he can. The Kick-ass Knight also leaves Alice with a curious, cryptic message about the importance of helmets as protective headgear. The knight warns of what is often an illusion of those wearing them to assume you'll be absolutely safe from any harm.

**The Lion**: The Lion ate the Unicorn, and coincidentally, was Dinah's distant cousin who contently called Africa jungles home. The Lion was known to be able to run very, very, very fast—in fact— faster than a unicorn.

**The Looking-Glass**: One of the two most reflective characters in this book.

**The Madd Hatter**: The abusively crazy,

telepathic owner of The Madd Hatter Bar & Restaurant (along with his wife, the Redd Queen). He's also Frottage Frank's brother-in-law.

**The Madd Hatter Bar & Restaurant**: The setting for most of the events that occur, and perhaps, is Alice's own personal purgatory.

**The Madd Hatter Bar & Restaurant Bouncers**: The hefty, husky gatekeepers who decide who gets into The Madd Hatter Bar & Restaurant, such as; party boys, party girls, paupers, princes, and princesses. They also act as security for The Madd Hatter and The Redd Queen and were the ones who dumped Dinah out on the street.

**The Mice**: The Mice are chased by Dinah in her dream but transform into giant insects when cornered, who then proceed to chase Dinah, turning her into a 'fraidy cat (although she's be ever so reluctant to admit that to anyone).

**The Mirror**: The other most reflective character in this book.

**The Pauper**: Apparently, a down-on-her-luck, destitute, homeless woman that Alice defends from The Madd Hatter Bar & Restaurant Bouncers (who also act as security for

The Madd Hatter and his wife, The Redd Queen). Taking a stand to protect The Pauper from Jude (one of the MHB&R bouncers), the waitress then bows and kneels before the soiled vagrant in an effort to help recover coins smacked from the woman's hand by a man with less than half a heart. Before letting The Pauper depart, Alice not only shares with her The Crown she's worn only for a brief time by placing it upon The Pauper's head but gives it to the unlucky lady to keep. Wait a minute! In reality, could The Pauper be—The White Queen—and/or the She who needs no introduction…

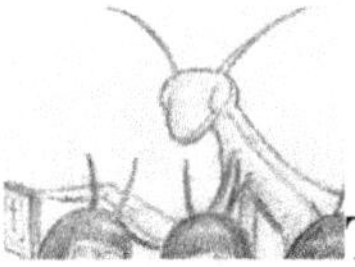

**The Praying Mantis**: A New King James version bible bearing bug who asks for forgiveness for all the things the bugs really could of, should of, and would have done better.

**The Reader**: A regular customer at The Madd Hatter Bar & Restaurant who earlier had casually befriended Alice, and then later becomes one of her confidants. The Reader, like Naida, also transmogrifies— not into a cat—but a rabbit; The White Rabbit, to be precise.

**The Redd Queen**: She's not only married to The Madd Hatter, but she's the co-owner of The Madd Hatter Bar & Restaurant. In addition, she's Frottage Frank's sister.

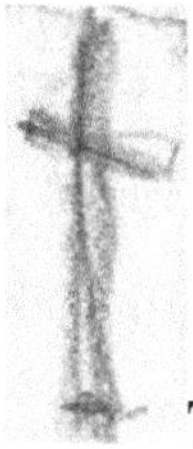

**The Son**: One of God's children who was hell-bent on saving those in need and whom She suspects may be suffering from a messiah complex or something. If only He had listened to His Mother!

**The Unicorn**: The unicorn was eaten by The Lion (coincidentally, one of Dinah's cousins, albeit a distant one in Africa). This would explain not only why The Madd Hatter Bar & Restaurant was all out of unicorns but also why we never see a unicorn anymore. The Unicorn was known to be able to run very, very, very fast—but sadly for The Unicorn—not faster than The Lion.

**The White Queen**: A woman at The Madd Hatter Bar & Restaurant dressed completely in white and wearing a beautiful crown. She and Alice become fast friends and gives the weary waitress two valuable tips before leaving. The coronated woman in white admits; she was an NYU Queen School dropout; she was wrong to bow to parental pressure to change her degree from English Lit to Queening; the lack of compatibility and communication with her recently deceased spouse, King William; and how she always wanted to be a poet. After abdicating the throne, The White Queen relinquished the use of "Your Majesty" as her title, to re-embrace and resume using her former, and more humble title of Pam the Poet.

**The White Rabbit**: The Reader, turned hare, who frequents The Madd Hatter Bar & Restaurant and casually befriends Alice. He's discovered the magical powers of books extend further than the knowledge to be enjoyed in them. Books, in a matter of speaking, also possess the ability to prevent unwanted people from talking to you, while also providing a literal cloak of invisibility to surreptitiously observe all that is around. He's not only notable for his ears and his care and concern for others, but also a tendency to be tardy.

**Tiger-lily**: One more *papier-mâché* flower.

**Violet**: The last of the *papier-mâché* flowers.

**Wee The People**: An exclusive, private club catering to the golden shower crowd. Frottage Frank is known to carry its VIP membership card in his wallet, and it's where he invited a hapless woman on a date with him to go for "drinks'.

# Acknowledgements and Dedication

Many thanks to The Madd Hatter Bar & Restaurant, located on Washington Street, in Hobohemia; my beloved adopted happy home. Special thanks go to Anja and Noika Weber, both of whom work at the Hatter, and who have offered much encouragement and inspiration (liquid and otherwise…) that went into writing this book. Without their care and kindness, I doubt it would've turned out the way it did. When initially sharing an idea for this tale, the plot was based upon an immigrant working as a waitress who had discovered that besides everything else life had thrown at her, she now also had to deal with an unplanned pregnancy. With their combined suggestions, the original character's name was changed to Alice and the setting to The Madd Hatter Bar & Restaurant. From there, everything just pretty much fell into place. And within eight days I had the first version of this book written; a book that literally felt like it wrote itself.

In the process of sharing those suggestions, Anja was behind the bar serving drinks while Noika had sidled up on the barstool next to me, curled up looking just like a cat. So, you can imagine in chapter two why the storyline took the unusual direction it did. I may not be the first to have said this (but if I am, then I'm proud to be that one); behind every good writer is great bartenders!

To set the record straight, this is a work of fantasy fiction, and it's not intended to cast aspersions upon the reputation or character, living or dead, of anyone who has, or who is, working at the Madd Hatter. Not the managers (and I'm not even sure if they have a night manager as mentioned in this work), and neither the staff nor the proprietor(s?). The segment depicted about the destitute woman is so far from the truth and just the opposite of what I've actually witnessed with my own eyes and ears while relaxing there. They appear to treat everyone equally well; with kindness and respect. Even yours truly…

Also, I bow in awe to the genius of Lewis Carroll, the author of many books that inspired not only his generation, but every generation to come afterward with the spark of imagination and childlike wonder of the world both seen and unseen that surrounds us; that world which some fail to see as being real. Particularly inspirational were his classic and iconic works: Alice's Adventures in Wonderland and Through the Looking-Glass.

Louie, baby, I couldn't have done this without you, you rascal!

At sixteen, Stevie B signed his first recording deal with a major label. Over the years he's produced records and composed songs for Madonna and other international artists. Since 2006 many of his music and book reviews have appeared in assorted entertainment publications. In 2012, "Pajamas on a Sun Stained Beach," his first published novel, hit the bookstores. That was followed by "The Freaky Fungal Family Tree" in 2021, as well as the upcoming "You're Crazy – I Love You!", "Chris and her Daughters", and "Beneath a Lazarus Moon." For nearly 40 years he's owned and managed Mia Mind Music, a successful entertainment promotion and marketing company that has accumulated multiple gold and platinum record awards in association with various record companies and artists. Born a be-freckled, bewildered, bemused, and bashful, blue-eyed boy from Baltimore, Maryland, he now resides contently alone in Hoboken,

New Jersey. In between publications, he offers short stories, thoughts, ramblings, and rants on his blog, www.thestevieb.com. Additional information also appears on his Facebook author page, www.facebook.com/thesteviebe.

www.ingramcontent.com/pod-product-compliance
Lightning Source LLC
LaVergne TN
LVHW012051160826
845678LV00014B/2787
*9798824008821*